Benton County
Rose

Sue Ellen Willett

PublishAmerica

Baltimore

First printing

All artwork is courtesy of: Sandy Rittgers.

ISBN: 1-59129-383-9
PUBLISHED BY PUBLISHAMERICA BOOK PUBLISHERS
www.publishamerica.com
Baltimore

Printed in the United States of America

Dedicated to Michael, Jacob, Janae & John

In memory of my parents

A special thank you to:

*my husband, Michael, for the many
ways in which you
contributed to this book.
Without you, this would not
have been possible.*

*Marilyn Baridon and Janae Willett for
their proofreading contributions,
Cecile Hoepfner for her contributions
to my music,
Leora Sauertag and Dr. Byron Kluss for
their historical contibutions,
and my children for their prayers.
Thank you PublishAmerica.*

SENTIMENTAL JOURNEY

Rose finished drying her hands by the kitchen sink after helping her mother do the dishes. They had just finished baking a red velvet cake. Today Rose was celebrating her sixteenth birthday, and it was going to be a birthday to remember!

"Rose, let's take a break while the cake is baking and go sit in the porch swing," said her mother. "I'd like to tell you a story about your grandparents as part of your birthday gift. I've been saving this surprise just for your sixteenth birthday."

"Grandmother Rose is the one that you named me after, right, Mother?" Rose perked up.

"Yes, that's right. You remind me of her more and more every day. You have her beautiful smile," said her mother.

"I don't remember my grandfather," said Rose.

"That's because he died when I was very young," said her mother. But your grandmother Rose did her best to keep his memory alive by telling me stories about him. I've been saving the best one for your sixteenth birthday. It begins when your grandmother was sixteen herself."

"Is Grandfather the one who fought in World War II?" asked Rose.

"Yes, and he became a war hero. The story is about your grandparents during World War II. You will want to pass it on to your children someday."

Mother wiped up the last bit of cake flour from the counter top. "Let's go now while the cake is baking and I'll tell you the story."

Rose immediately rushed out to the porch and dropped into the swing. Her mother quickly followed after retrieving a small package from the bedroom.

Lowering herself into the swing next to Rose, her mother said, "Did you know that your grandparents actually sat in this very swing when they first met?"

"This was their swing?" asked Rose.

"Well, it belonged to your great-grandparents," said her mother, as she gently pushed the porch floor with her feet to begin a gentle swinging motion.

"How long has this farm been in our family?" asked Rose

"Oh lets see now…" Her mother stopped to think a moment. "It's been in the family for 150 years. It's now called a century farm."

"We're lucky to live here!" said Rose.

"Yes we are," her mother agreed. "Maybe you can pass it on to your family someday."

"Just like the cake recipe and all of your stories," said Rose.

"That's right!" her mother agreed. "There is so much family history here. Let's get started before our time is up. After the cake cools we can frost it together. Now, I'm going to tell you the story of how your grandmother became the Rose of Benton County…"

CHAPTER 1: BEAUTIFUL DREAMER

The year was 1941. School was just about finished for the summer. Just a mile west of town, on a dusty county road, a bus door opened. With a great burst of energy, out rushed a young woman named Rose Krueger. Rose was a sixteen-year-old girl that lived on a farm just outside of a small town in Iowa called Apple Grove.

She ran down the long gravel driveway as fast as she could go. Along beside her, nipping at her ankles, chased her spunky dog named Herkimer. Herkimer was her very best friend in the world. When Rose would get home from school, he greeted her faithfully. It was as if he instinctively knew each day the exact time the school bus would arrive out in front of the farmhouse. Herk was there and waiting like a reliable old habit.

Rose pulled back her thick brown hair adorned in soft curls that framed her heart-shaped face, and she reached over to pet Herk.

"Hello old friend!" she gently spoke, greeting Herk with her movie star smile. "How was your day here at the farm?"

Her big brown eyes met his. Herk wagged his tail back and forth and jiggled around with great excitement.

Rose continued to run down the long lane and past the green water pump in the front of the two-story farmhouse and into the east door. The screen slammed behind her and bounced off the frame a few times before finally settling to a close.

"Mother, where are you?" Rose called out. "Guess what happened to me at school today?"

"I'm upstairs," called her mother, Grace. "You'll have to come up here to talk to me."

Rose ran down the hallway and swung her arm around the vast banister that trimmed the ornate staircase to climb the steep steps. She skipped every other one until she reached the top.

"Guess what, Mother?"

"What is it, Rose?"

"The senior class has nominated me to run for Benton County Sweet Corn Queen!" Rose tried to explain while catching her breath.

"At the September Sweet Corn Festival?" asked Mother.

"Yes, that's right!" replied Rose.

"We'll have to get ready for it over the summer," said Mother. "You don't have anything proper to wear for it."

"I can make myself a new dress," said Rose.

"Out of what," asked Mother?

"Well, I don't know," she said. "Maybe I could use the fabric from the old curtains that you saved from the living room."

"The old fabric from the living room curtains!" Mother cried out. "You are so creative Rose, but don't be ridiculous!"

"Why sure," said Rose. "We have to make do and re-use things right now, don't we? Times are tough, aren't they?"

"Yes, but what will other people think?" asked Mother.

"I don't care what other people think, Mother," answered Rose. "I think it's very pretty!"

"Oh, that just won't do Rose," her mother demanded. "You'll have to work harder to sell more eggs, and then you can go into town to one of the general stores and buy some new fabric."

"OK Mother," Rose agreed. "If you insist. I was just trying to be practical like you always want me to be. Maybe I'll even have enough money left over to buy some more bobby pins to do my hair in pin curls the night before the contest."

"Pin curls!" Her mother let out a sigh. "You are not going to fix your hair in pin curls for this event."

"But Mother, that's how I always fix it. I like it that way!"

"Rose, this is a very special occasion. You'll need to perm your hair for this," said her mother. "I can put the perm in for you. Just buy one in town when you get your new fabric."

Grace was a very devoted mother with a saintly polish, and it appeared that God had found favor in her daughter, Rose, and blessed her with elegance and beauty beyond her years.

"Tell me more about the queen contest while I finish folding your laundry," said her mother.

"Maybe we could go to Cedar City to get fabric," said Rose.

"No, it takes most of the day to travel there on the train," said her mother. "We'd have to stay over night, and that would cost too much money. You should be able to find some fabric that you like in town here. We're lucky to have two general stores to shop from. Just remember not to get carried away with your dress. Keep it simple and make it have the versatility to be used for other occasions."

"Oh Mother, you care way too much about what other people think! Just for one night I'd like to wear something that wasn't so practical. In fact, I'd like it to be stunning and I'd like it to be all my own idea!"

"I'm just trying to teach you how to dress appropriately for the occasion," said Mother. "And keep in mind our current circumstances. Times are hard. We are experiencing a depression in the economy. A special occasion dress is just not on our list of priorities right now. Your father is worried about just being able to hang onto the farm. Why we don't even know where the money for your college education will come from!"

"All the more reason to use the old curtain fabric that I like so well," Rose suggested again.

"Yes, I suppose that's true, but if you sell your own eggs to buy new fabric we'll both be happy," said Mother. "Oh Rose, why can't you be like the other girls in Apple Grove!"

"Mother, what do you mean?"

"They are simple country girls that have just three goals in life, the desire to get confirmed in the church, to graduate and to get married."

"I'm not like all the other girls," Rose retaliated. "I have only shared one goal with all of those other girls, and that was to get confirmed in the Lutheran church. The rest of my goals in life are very different from theirs. You can't punish me for desiring more in life and having far greater dreams than my friends."

Rose turned away from her mother, her shoulders drooping and her head looking down toward the floor.

"I'm not like the other girls here, Mother. I don't fit in. I've felt it for a long time. Even in the church. I don't know if I can adopt the strict Lutheran ways, Mother. I feel a lot of pressure to conform just to please you and Father. I just don't know if I can live up to your expectations in those areas."

"Why, Rose Krueger! You ought to be ashamed of yourself and those thoughts about the church!" Her mother put her hand over her mouth.

"You know, Mother, there are other churches that are just as good."

"Why, Rose, you know that if your not a Lutheran that...well...you know."

"I know what?" Rose asked.

"Well I can't even talk about it!"

Rose threw up her hands and shook her head in disbelief of what she was hearing. She certainly hadn't intended for this conversation to get out of control like this. She felt that this was not the time or the place to argue about her Lutheran heritage. Rose loved her mother very much, but she wasn't like her in that sense. In fact, she wasn't like her in a lot of ways. She had her own individual style, and she wanted to express her own personality, which was very different from her mothers.

"I've got to talk to Father. Where is he?" asked Rose as she became very anxious to end the conversation.

"He's out in the barn milking the cows," said Grace.

"I think I'll go find him," said Rose as she quickly headed for the stairs.

Rose slid down the banister to the bottom of the stairs, and she ran down the hall and out the kitchen door to the barn.

"Father, where are you? I need to talk to you," she called.

"I'm over here Rose," her father said as he looked up from underneath a cow that he was trying to milk. "How was your day at school?"

"I've got some exciting new!" she said. "I've been chosen to run for Benton County Sweet Corn Queen!"

"That's wonderful!" he said as he got out from underneath the large milking cow. He picked her up in his strong arms and hugged her. "I'm very proud of you!"

Her father, Conrad, was a big stocky man with a warm smile. He was the fifth top producing dairy farmer in the state of Iowa.

"If that will make you happy, Rose, go for it!" said her father with a reassuring nod of approval. "That's my girl!" He gave her a loving pat on the back.

"I'm going to design my own dress for the contest and I'm planning to go into town for the materials," said Rose.

"Did your mother approve that?" he asked.

"Yes, we have covered the issue at great length," said Rose.

"And just how can we afford to buy fabric?"

"I'm going to sell eggs in town to raise the money. Don't worry. I know that money is scarce right now. I'll take care of it."

"Sounds good," he said. "Have fun!"

Rose ran back toward the house stopping halfway to pick a daisy. She flung herself around in a circle as she danced with excitement as if the world belonged only to her.

The view from her upstairs bedroom was magnificent. It was a special place for special dreams.

Dreams were something that Rose was very familiar with. She spent many hours in her room just dreaming of the day when she would be able to leave the farm and the country life. She dreamed of going far away from home and the small town of Apple Grove that she was so familiar with.

There were times when she thought that if she had to spend one more day in that house, or in that room, or in that bed that she would just wither up and die. Why she often felt that way was confusing to her. Her family was very loving and all. But she wanted to experience more in life—beyond the farm, beyond Apple Grove and beyond Iowa.

These feelings lingered in the shadow of her dreams that were becoming more and more frequent.

ക'ക'ക

From her upstairs bedroom, you could see miles and miles of rolling hills and lush, green trees and cornfields filled with perfectly shaped corn stalks. The view was an invitation to daydream and to carefully work out life's details and plans for the future. And Rose had big plans for the future!

A soft breeze from the nearby grove of trees blew in the west window, and the summer sun kissed the windowsill while the curtains gently danced around.

This is my favorite place in the whole world, thought Rose. I can be anybody and do anything in this special place. I have so many dreams, but first I want to be crowned queen for a day.

I can just imagine having a beautiful dress with soft pink lace that flows to the floor in the most romantic way. It could have a cinched waistline with a gathered bodice, a round neckline, and a double-puffed sleeve. It could be embellished with sweetheart roses on each side of the neckline. Roses have to be somewhere on the dress. They're my favorite flowers. Yes! That's it! This would be the perfect gown for a perfect evening! My room never fails me. It is where I get the inspiration for all of my dreams!

Off she went to share her idea for her dress with her often-skeptical parents. Her mother and father were very conservative and traditional farmers who sometimes only shook their heads at her big ideas and her very strong desire to carry them out. They often reminded her that she was a simple farmer's daughter, and that simplicity was always best.

Rose went downstairs to the kitchen table to lay out her plans and show them to her parents. Her father had finished up his chores, and he had just come inside.

"What do you think of my plans for my dress?" asked Rose.

"Looks good to me!" said her father as he quickly glanced over the plans.

"It looks as if you could cut it off later to wear to church on Sundays," her mother observed. "Oh, and before I forget to tell you, Wayne called."

"Do I need to call him back?"

"No. He just asked me to remind you to pack some food for your date."

"Oh, that's right! We're going on a picnic! I got so carried away thinking about making this dress that I totally forgot!"

"Where are you two going on your picnic?" asked her mother.

"We're going to Hidden Lake. We'll also be picking up Lilly and her friend Ben."

Lilly and Rose were best friends. Lilly lived just down the road, and they both had a lot in common. They went a lot of places together and spent a great deal of time riding their horses down the gravel road. Lilly was just about as close to having a real sister as Rose could get. They were inseparable until Wayne Johnson came along.

Rose went into the pantry off the kitchen and brought out a picnic basket. She quickly gathered items from the pantry and carefully placed them in the basket. She covered the top of the basket with a red and white-checkered tablecloth and made her way to the kitchen door.

"Don't be late," said her father.

"Don't worry, I won't! I'll see you later," said Rose as she went out the door with her basket hanging from her arm.

Rose had been dating a young man by the name of Wayne Johnson for quite some time now. Wayne was an easy-going guy, very polite, and very caring. His biggest ambition in life was to stay at home after he graduated from high school and farm with his father. This was a questionable ambition to Rose. She wanted much more out of life, and she had big dreams that didn't quite match up with his.

Wayne enjoyed the simple pleasures in life like nature, long walks, and picnics with friends. He wasn't very athletic, but he was very well read. He would go on talking for hours about literature that he had reviewed and how he was going to change the way his father farmed once he got involved.

Wayne Johnson had completely fallen for beautiful and adventurous Rose. He considered himself the luckiest guy in the world to be dating her, even though they were very different from one another, and they had very different dreams for the future. But Rose's parents highly approved of Wayne. He was a nice Lutheran boy, from a nice Lutheran family, who attended the Lutheran school in town, and he loved farming, just like her father.

Wayne drove down the farmhouse lane and beeped the horn three times as usual for Rose to come out. Off they went to pick up their friends to enjoy a special outing that was very typical of their dates.

They rolled down the windows and enjoyed the soft summer night breeze as they traveled down the dusty road that led to the lake.

Hidden Lake was nestled in the eastern part of Benton County, tucked way back in the countryside snuggled in between the rolling hills of Iowa farmland. It had a nice beach area where they all began their evening with a swim.

No motorboats were allowed on the lake, so it remained very calm and peaceful. It was a great place to kick back and relax. For the most part, they all enjoyed swimming there, and the view of the hills and the trees surrounding the lake were magnificent around this quaint little lake.

"I love to swim!" said Wayne. "This feels so good."

"I don't care for it much," Rose retorted. "I can only do one stroke well."

Rose began to demonstrate the only stroke that she knew how to do. That stroke was the side-stroke. She gracefully stretched out her arms on top of the water and took off in what seemed like a smooth glide for about 10 feet. Then, she suddenly stopped as if she began to become fearful.

She stood up onto her feet and announced, "I'm getting hungry from all of this swimming."

"Me too," agreed Wayne. "What did you bring along to eat, Rose? Something fancy or something simple just the way I like it?"

"This time I aimed to please you, Wayne. I brought plain old hot dogs to roast over a fire."

"You two are so different from one another. How did you ever get together?" asked Ben.

"Rose appears to have different views on things, but she eventually comes around to my way of thinking," teased Wayne.

Rose gave a piercing glance at Wayne and said, "I might not always come around, much less be around!"

"You two just stop it, and let's get on up to the top of the hill and start a campfire," suggested Lilly. "I'm getting hungry."

"Me too," agreed Rose.

They made their way up to the shelter area on top of the hill overlooking the lake. Wayne and Ben worked together to build a nice roaring fire. The girls found some long sticks nearby to roast the hot dogs on.

This was the way that Wayne liked it. He enjoyed a simple date with friends and Rose. There was just one problem—Rose was far from simple!

Wayne took Rose home last. As he slowly walked her up to the door, he took her hand and turned her to face him.

"Rose, I have something for you," he said as he spoke soft and seriously.

"What is it, Wayne?"

"Here, Rose," he said as he took her hand in his. He carefully slid a ring onto her finger. "I'd like you to wear this."

Rose looked at her hand and then at his face, "Your class ring?"

"Yes, I'd really like you to have it!"

"Wayne, what does this mean?" she asked as she looked into his eyes.

Wayne could sense that Rose was beginning to feel uncomfortable. He looked directly back into her beautiful brown eyes and said, "It means that we're going steady. That we are exclusively dating one another."

Rose broke eye contact and said, "I—I guess that would be OK for now. I've got to go. It's getting late."

"Goodnight Rose."

"Goodnight Wayne."

Rose turned and ran into the house a bit taken by this. She wasn't sure what to think and what their relationship really meant. She preferred not to make a big issue out of it just yet. She was still confused about what she wanted for the future.

⁂

The following week school dismissed for summer, and Rose spent a good share of her time selling eggs in town. She finally raised enough money to go shopping for fabric.

It was a beautiful Saturday morning. Rose and her mother got up early to go into town to shop. They took Conrad's old Mercury, which he had driven for a number of years now. It had some miles stacked up on it, but it ran like a charm, and it was extremely reliable.

As they were driving into town, Rose looked over at her mother and said, "I've got something to tell you."

"What is it Rose?"

"Wayne gave me his class ring."

"Oh," said Grace with a raised eyebrow. "Is it getting serious?"

"Yes, I think so. I think that Wayne is swell, but I still want to go out east after I graduate. Wayne wants to stay here in Apple Grove and help his father farm. I don't know what I'm going to tell him."

"He wants you to stay here too?"

"Yes, I think so."

"Well, I think that you should," her mother quickly agreed.

"But Mother, you know how I dream to go out east."

"You still have plenty of time to decide on your plans for after high school," said her mother. "You have a whole year left before you graduate. We have a lot to work out before then. Your future is as uncertain as our finances are right now."

"I realize that, but I'm not giving up on my dreams yet!"

"Well, give it some more thought and then tell him what you would like to do when the time is right," said her mother. "He's a very nice Lutheran young man! He'd make a great husband someday."

Rose looked at her mother out of the corner of her eye, and it became very quiet in the car. Rose thought about Wayne and their future. Her mother could sense her daughter's worry, so she decided to leave her alone with her thoughts.

They arrived in downtown Apple Grove. Rose and her mother shopped in both stores until they found everything that they needed to make the dress. Rose even had enough money left over to buy a permanent wave, which her mother put in for her the next day.

Rose spent many long hours working on her dress for the festival until it was completed to her satisfaction. The skills Rose had learned in 4-H about sewing had paid off. She was trying on her dress in her upstairs bedroom when she heard a knock at the door.

"Come in."

"Hi!" said Wayne appearing in the doorway.

"Wayne, you startled me!"

"Wow! Don't you look stunning!"

"Speaking of stunning, you just stunned me! How did you get past my mother?"

"I knocked, but no one came to the door, so I just let myself in."

"If my parents find you up here, I'll be in a heap of trouble, Wayne Johnson!"

"I'm sorry, Rose. I thought that your parents liked me."

"They do," replied Rose. "It's just that they are very strict with their rules concerning dating. They're old-fashioned!"

"I like your folks. We see things eye-to-eye," he said.

"That's for sure!" Rose agreed. "That's just the problem. You all think alike and I think differently, but I don't want to go into that now. I just had a discussion about that with my mother the other day and I wished that I hadn't brought it up.

"Since you're already up here what do you think?" Rose asked as she twirled around in front of him standing there in the doorway.

"You look like a million bucks!" answered Wayne. He couldn't take his eyes off her.

"I'll meet you back downstairs, Wayne. Let me change and then we can take a walk. There is something I need to talk to you about."

After Rose changed her clothes and came downstairs, she grabbed Wayne by the hand and led him outside. They walked down the long driveway and across the road to the field. Continuing to walk hand-in-hand, they crossed the field and climbed to the top of a hill. It was a beautiful summer day, and the air smelled like freshly cut grass with the sweet smell of clover and honeysuckle that was softly being carried by a gentle breeze.

They decided to stop on top of the hill to talk. Rose spread out a beautiful quilt, and they both sat down to enjoy the view. You could look out over many acres of farmland. It overlooked the entire family farm.

"Just look at your father's massive barn," said Wayne as he pointed to it down below.

"It's the largest barn in Iowa, my father tells me."

"I think that it very well could be," said Wayne as he looked to admire the structure.

"Look at the cemetery over there on the other hill. That's where most of my relatives are buried," explained Rose. "That includes my Grandfather and Grandmother Krueger, and my Great-Grandfather and Great-Grandmother Krueger. The tallest stone that you can see from here is my great-grandfather's, who came over from Germany. He bought our farm back in 1854. Many of my relatives have lived in the farmhouse at one time or another. That's why this farm and this land are so special to us."

"I can see why," said Wayne. "You're a close family."

"Just like your family, Wayne. That's why we would make such a great couple," said Rose as she reached out for his hand. "There's just one problem…"

"What is it Rose?" asked Wayne eager to know what was wrong.

"Well, I have plans—big plans, Wayne. I'd like to go out east after I graduate and attend nursing school."

"I see," replied Wayne, sounding disappointed.

He paused for a moment and then turned her toward himself and said, "I'll wait for you. I'm staying here on the farm to help my father, but when you're finished with school, we'll get married! I'll wait however long it takes. There's no one else for me, Rose—only you!"

Rose put her head down softly on his shoulder.

Wayne drew her close, and they sat together for a while and watched the sun set from high up on the hill over-looking the family farm.

There were no more words to say.

CHAPTER 2: GAZEBO WALTZ

Rose got up early to help her father with the 8:00 AM milking in the barn. Fall and the long awaited day of the Benton County Sweet Corn Festival had arrived. Conrad milked his eighty head of cattle three times a day. He milked at 8:00am, 4:00pm, and then finished up at midnight. Rose enjoyed getting up to help with the milking once in awhile. She admired her father's strength and his dedication to his work. She enjoyed visiting with him and learning from him as often as she could. He told interesting stories. He usually had a story problem for her to figure out that always contained a trick question.

Conrad was a busy man raising his dairy cattle and three hundred head of hogs and raising grain for the livestock on their farm. But on this day of September 1941, he was excited for his daughter. He planned to get his work finished early so that he could go to the festival in Vinceton.

"Father, I'm very nervous about today," said Rose as they stood next to one another in the barn.

"You'll do just fine," her father smiled as he swept his brow under his black cap. "You are the prettiest farmer's daughter in Iowa!"

"Oh Father, that's ridiculous!"

" No, it's not. I know it's true because I saw all the girls at the last state 4-H convention when you were President. You stood up and addressed the entire group with more poise and finesse than all of those girls put together!"

"You're just saying this because I'm your daughter."

"And a very special one at that!" said Conrad. "I think that you should go in now and eat your mother's breakfast and get ready. I'll finish up here by myself. Run along."

"I love you!" Rose said as she gave her father a big hug.

Out the barn door she went and into the farmhouse kitchen. Her mother was setting the breakfast table with their very best dishes. They were decorated with dainty pink pastel flowers. These dishes had been in the family for along time. They had also belonged to her great-grandmother.

The kitchen was filled with the smell of fresh German apple pancakes. This was a favorite family tradition from Grandmother Krueger. These were only made on very special occasions like this one. Rose could sense that her parents were supportive of her. This helped her to feel more confident.

"Mother, thanks for this special breakfast," said Rose as she sat down at the big kitchen table that was so carefully decorated. "It looks so delicious!"

"You're welcome. I'm so excited that you are running for Sweet Corn Queen. I thought we should celebrate! I can hardly wait!" said her mother.

"These pancakes taste so good," commented Rose as she dove into the hot stack. "Do you think that I have a chance to win?"

"Winning or losing is not the issue, Rose."

"Yes, but what will everyone think of me if I lose?"

"We'll all love you just the same whether you win or lose," said her mother reassuringly.

"I know, but it would still be nice to win."

"Just be yourself and enjoy the experience," her mother encouraged. " I'll do your chores for you today."

"That would be great! I guess it's time for me to get ready," said Rose as she looked at her watch."

"It's your special day Rose. Enjoy it!"

Rose finished up her breakfast and excused herself from the kitchen to go to her room. She found it difficult to concentrate on getting her things together. She felt muddled and disorganized as she paced around the room trying to clarify her needs. She had a hard time trying to decide what to wear and what to take with her. She even found it difficult to decide what makeup colors to wear and how to style her hair. She finally gave in and called her mother up to help her with some of these decisions and found that she was very anxious to give her opinion. Rose actually found it helpful to just let go and let her mother take over. She was able to pull things together in a very orderly way.

"Rose, Wayne is coming up the driveway," her mother noticed as she glanced out the window from the bedroom.

"I'm just about ready."

"It's 11:15, Rose, and the festival starts at noon!"

"I know, Mother. I'm trying to hurry."

"It takes about forty-five minutes to get there," added Grace.

"I know Mother, I just have to do one more thing!"

Wayne arrived on time as usual to pick up Rose. Rose raced down the staircase swinging her arm around the banister with her clothing bag wrapped around her arm.

"I'll see you at the festival, Mother," Rose called out as she dashed out the back door.

She was wearing her best casual clothes. Her new dress was neatly packed in a plastic zip- up clothing bag that she carried in her hand for the contest.

Wayne got out of the car and came around to open up the door for Rose.

"You're just on time as usual," commented Rose.

"Let's eat lunch there," suggested Wayne.

"My stomach doesn't feel so good," said Rose.

"That's normal."

"I'll be glad when this is all over," she said.

"You'll do great, Rose."

"I hope that you are right!"

While driving to Vinceton, Wayne could sense that Rose was very nervous, so he tried to calm her down by telling her some jokes. It only worked for a while. They arrived just in time to hear the noon whistle blow.

Sweet Corn Days was a festival that was held every fall in the largest town in the county, known as the county seat. It officially began at noon with the sounding of the fire whistle from the fire station. Wayne especially enjoyed this sound for he was training to become a volunteer fireman. He wanted to serve the community in this capacity after he graduated from high school and began farming with his father. The whistle blew every day at noon like clockwork. Everyone in town knew when it was lunchtime. The businesses closed up here for the lunch hour just like they did in all of the smaller towns around the area.

People were beginning to gather in the Town Square out in front of the courthouse, greeting one another with warm smiles. Everyone seemed to know each other. Many of them were related in some way, whether it be first cousins, second cousins or on down the line. Families, friends, and the Sweet Corn Festival were an important part of September in Iowa. People regarded this as the last big event before the harvest and the close of summer.

The park surrounding the Town Square was a glorious sight. The flowers were magnificent and in full bloom. The town garden club meticulously kept them up. This was their time of the year to shine.

The park was filled with the reddest geraniums ever, Queen Elizabeth roses in pastel pink, gladiolus in mixed colors, and orange lilies. Fragrant Sweet William in large clusters bordered the rocks around the park.

A beautiful gazebo sat on the north side of the park. It was outlined by bleeding hearts in locket-shaped blooms with graceful arching stems. This added a touch of romance to the park.

There was a stage set up in the Town Square for entertainment. Some of the events included a talent show, solos, dancing by the town cloggers, bluegrass bands, folk singers, etc...the grand finale was the crowning of the Sweet Corn Queen.

Food venders stretched on all sides of the Town Square offering many homemade delicacies. They offered barbecue beef sandwiches, potato salad, every kind of homemade pie that you could think of, and freshly squeezed lemonade. But the big attraction that pulled in people for miles around was the sweet corn.

Troughs full of sweet corn and big boiling pots were set up. Truckloads of sweet corn were shucked, boiled, and served golden yellow with loads of butter melted on top. People waited in long lines that wrapped around the park for this final taste of Iowa summer. Children ran around barefoot, laughing and playing while their parents ate at picnic tables visiting with friends. The entertainment on the stage went on the entire day and well into the evening and was enjoyed by all.

Rose and Wayne filled their plates with delicious foods and planted themselves down under a shade tree to eat and listen to the music on center stage.

"Look Wayne. Here come my folks."

"Who's with them?"

"My aunts and uncles."

"I see. Look over by the sweet corn line. There are your 4-H friends."

"Oh yes, there's Lilly, Dorothy, Marian and Beverly."

"Maybe they'll come join us," he said.

"If they don't, I'll go talk to them after I eat," said Rose as she slowly worked away at all of the food that was piled up on her plate.

Rose was a very slow eater. She was always the last one to finish. She enjoyed her food and often commented on every item that she ate.

Rose and Wayne were very comfortable eating under the shade tree there in the park, delighting in the entertainment on the stage and greeting people as they walked by. It was a very enjoyable time, and Rose finally found herself relaxing.

After they had finished eating, Rose got up, threw her paper plate in the nearby trash barrel, and said to Wayne, "I'm going to go visit with my friends for awhile. I'll meet up with you later."

Rose found her 4-H friends. They were all very close. Rose was the current President of the Benton County chapter. She enjoyed 4-H leadership and found it rewarding when membership had significantly increased after she became President. Rose was a very responsible and hard working farm girl.

"Hi Rose," said Lilly. "Did you happen to see this really handsome guy walking around here?"

"No, not yet," said Rose

Dorothy chimed in "He's so tall, dark and…"

"Handsome!" Marion added.

"He's really swell!" Beverly blurted out. "He came with Lilly's folks."

"So Lilly, who is this swell guy that's with your folks?" asked Rose as she nudged her with her elbow.

"He's staying with us and he's…"

"Staying with you?" interrupted Beverly.

"Yes, he's staying with us," Lilly went on trying to explain. "He's a banker from Baltimore."

"Baltimore?" Rose responded with interest.

"Yes, and he has come out here to the Mid-West to try to purchase farmland."

"Why would he want to purchase farmland?" asked Dorothy.

"I suppose for an investment, but I'm not really sure. My parents are pretty secretive about that part."

" I've heard some say that he's going to purchase the local bank," said Dorothy.

"Well, I don't know anything about that," said Lilly. "But my folks are major stockholders in the bank. That's why he is staying with us."

"You're lucky Lilly!" said Marion

"Rose, keep your eyes out for a very handsome stranger," teased Beverly.

"I guess I'll have to," chuckled Rose. "You've all made him sound very fascinating."

"Oh, and Rose, check out the flowers that are in full bloom around the gazebo," suggested Lilly.

"Are they the ones that our 4-H club donated this year?" asked Marian.

"They should be," said Rose. "I have a record of our club paying for them from the Treasurer."

As 4-H president, Rose learned to be a meticulous record-keeper. She also learned this from her father, who kept very detailed records for his dairy farm operation.

"The flowers by the gazebo are grand," added Lilly. "We all wish you luck today. We hope you win!"

The girls gathered around Rose with lots of enthusiasm, and they gave her a hug. They all thought highly of Rose.

Rose made her way over to the gazebo to closely view the flower project. She carefully touched the bleeding hearts at the entryway. They were stunning.

Just as she reached down to pull the arching stem closer to her nose, a voice from behind her softly spoke.

"The flowers are very beautiful!"

Rose turned her head upward to quickly see who was there. On the bench inside the gazebo was a man. He appeared to be very tall and slender. His eyes were warm and his smile was friendly.

"Yes, the flowers are very beautiful," replied Rose. "My 4-H club donated these for a community project this year to help beautify this park."

The man stood to his feet, and he held out his hand.

"I'm Adam Waterman."

Rose offered her hand to meet his.

"I'm Rose. Rose Krueger that is."

"Rose. What a beautiful name."

"Thank you," she answered as her face reddened.

29

"Sorry if I startled you. I was just sitting here admiring the flowers in this park."

"That's all right." Rose answered still a little shaken. "I wasn't expecting anyone to be sitting in here, I guess. Are you here to enjoy the festival?"

"Yes, I was invited to come with some people that I am..."

"Staying with," finished Rose.

"Yes, how did you know?"

"Oh, just a hunch I guess."

"That's a pretty good hunch. I'm here on business from..."

"From Baltimore," Rose interjected.

"Right again! Now how is it that you know so much about me?" he asked.

Rose grinned. "I just happen to be good friends with the daughter of the folks that you're staying with. She's here and she just told me about you."

"Oh, that explains it. Is that Lilly?"

"Yes."

"Nice girl."

"We're very good friends. Best friends."

"That's nice. I have a best friend back in Maryland too. We played college football together."

"So you're athletic?"

"I guess you could say that. How about you?"

"No—not me. I have other interests."

"Like 4-H club?"

"Yes, I guess so."

Feeling a little uncomfortable about where this conversation was going or how to end it without making herself look foolish, Rose felt the urgent need to escape the situation.

"It was nice to meet you. I hope that you enjoy your stay. I need to get back to my friend, I mean friends."

Rose turned away, quickly excusing herself. She felt a little flush. She couldn't recall ever seeing a man that looked like he did around Benton County. He was dressed up in a smart-looking tailored suit.

The young men in Benton County usually only wore jeans and flannel shirts, except to church on Sundays. Her father always wore overalls.

The stranger was a breath of fresh air, and Rose felt a bit taken back by her feelings. Her thoughts began to wander. He must be much older than I, and he's from a very different part of the country. This was a part of the country that she wanted to get to know more about. This seemed strange to suddenly meet someone from the part of the country where she wanted to go to college.

She thought about trying to find him again and talking to him more about Maryland, but she had a lot on her mind, and after all, she was with Wayne. She quickly dismissed the idea and found her friends.

Late afternoon arrived, and it was time for the queen candidates to begin getting ready for the contest. Rose gathered her dress and sought out the dressing room in the nearby building.

Her hands were sweating so profusely that she could hardly button her own dress. The pressure was mounting.

It came time for the contest to begin. The Master of Ceremonies called out the names of each contestant as she walked out onto the stage. He read something about each girl as they took turns walking out.

"Rose Krueger," he announced. "Miss Krueger is the daughter of Mr. and Mrs. Conrad Krueger of Apple Grove. She is a member of the 1942 high school graduating class. Rose is the President of her 4-H Club and has been in the club for six years. She has served as President, Secretary, Treasurer, Historian, and News Reporter. County recognitions in 4-H work for Miss Krueger have included five years of perfect attendance, six-year personal expense account book, a six year record memory book contest, state candidate for a New York trip, and representative at conservation camp for three years. Rose takes part in many social activities and social affairs at school. Benton County is proud of this farmer's daughter, Rose Krueger!"

Rose gracefully walked across the front of the stage in her beautiful gown that she had made. She was all smiles and waves.

She had a lot of experience being up in front of people in her 4-H leadership roles. Rose carried herself with great confidence.

The contest was mainly a beauty pageant. There was no talent involved, but the girls were asked one personal question that carried a lot of weight with the judges. Rose was the last one to be questioned.

The Master of Ceremonies walked over to Rose with the microphone and addressed her with this question, "Miss Krueger, what was the most enjoyable 4-H project that you have done in the past and what have you learned from it?"

"I was lucky enough to be able to attend a 4-H conservation camp last summer as a representative from our group. For a camp project, I put together a conservation book. As part of this project I learned the names of many kinds of trees and birds. I made a birdhouse and I became very good at identifying trees by looking at their leaves. I enjoyed making our home more beautiful by planting trees, making a gladiolus bed, and planting many other kinds of flowers. I also learned to identify weeds, which I found very interesting. I learned about soil conservation and soil erosion by making maps of our farm and found it very helpful to have my father explain the land to me. I learned many new things."

"Sounds like you did a lot of activities for this project," the M.C. commented.

"Yes, and I think that every girl should learn about conservation, even if she does not have the privilege of going to a 4-H camp. It taught me to appreciate more things around me and how I, as a member of society, can help by supporting all legislation concerning conservation. I also learned how farmers could help by cooperating with government conservation agencies in all of their efforts, and then on their own, following approved methods of crop rotation and conservation."

"Wow! Sounds great, Miss Krueger," said the M.C. "I bet that your father is proud of you! Thank you and you may take your place with the rest of the girls."

Rose joined the rest of the candidates, and they all lined up in the middle of the stage in a row. They joined hands in anticipation of the judge's decision. The panel of judges sat down in the right hand corner in front of the stage. The judges consisted of five well-known people from the community such as the mayor, the sheriff, the banker, the town doctor, and the garden club president.

The Master of Ceremonies opened the envelope with the winner's name on it. Rose took one last glance through the audience. She spotted her folks in the very front row. Wayne was near the center with Lilly and the gals. Her eyes caught sight of the easterner back off to the right of the stage leaning up against a tree with his hands in his pockets. Her gaze briefly met his. She looked into his eyes for a moment hoping that he wouldn't notice. He did notice, and he smiled at her as if she had his vote. She smiled back with acceptance and then looked back at the M.C. just in time to hear the decision.

"This year's Benton County Sweet Corn Queen is Miss Rose Krueger! Congratulations to you, Rose!" said the M.C.

There was a spectacular applause of approval from the audience. She was definitely the favorite. Everyone cheered as Rose became Benton County Sweet Corn Queen on that memorable September day in Iowa.

The band began to play and the Queen and her court were given the first dance of the evening. Wayne came over to dance with Rose. Everyone soon joined in with his or her partner.

After they had danced awhile, Wayne felt someone tap him on the shoulder from behind.

It was Ed, a fireman from Apple Grove. Apparently, a big barn fire had broken out near town, and they needed him to pitch in and help.

"I'm sorry Rose, I have to go."

"That's OK. I understand," she said trying to hide her disappointment.

"I might not make it back."

"I'll get a ride with my folks."

"Try to find your friends. You can hang out with them."

"I will."

"You were great today, Rose. Congratulations! I've got to run," he said quickly leaving with Ed.

Rose began to look around for her friends. The crowd was thick, and it was beginning to get dark. She couldn't seem to find her friends anywhere, so she decided to look in the gazebo.

As she walked into the doorway of the gazebo she saw Mr. Waterman sitting there on the bench. This reminded her of a few hours ago when she first met him there before the contest.

"Back again, Mr. Waterman?"

"And you, Miss Krueger?"

"I was just trying to find my friends. What are you doing here?"

"I like sitting in here. It's so relaxing and the flowers smell so good. Besides, I don't know very many people."

"I suppose so," she agreed. "Did you enjoy the contest?"

"Yes, you did great. Congratulations!"

"Thanks. It was a lot of work, but I guess it was all worth it."

"Would you like to sit down and join me here for awhile?"

"Sure."

Rose sat down and they both listened to the band from inside the gazebo for quite some time. They enjoyed just watching the people and visiting with one another.

"This band is good," Mr. Waterman commented.

"I agree." said Rose. "They have been playing some of my favorite songs, like *Dark Town Strutter's Ball*. That's a good song to dance to. You can really kick up your heels!"

"I really liked, *Let Me Call You Sweetheart* and *I'm Getting Sentimental Over You*. I guess I prefer the slow songs."

The M.C. announced that they would be playing the last song of the evening, a slow waltz that was dedicated to all of the girls that had participated in the queen contest.

"Rose, do you like to dance?"

"Yes, I do."

"May I have this last dance?"

"Right here? In the gazebo?"

"Yes. Right here."

"Sure, why not."

Adam gently wrapped his arm around her tiny waist and held her hand with the other as they slowly began to waltz. They danced as if they had danced together before. Every step that they took was together and smooth like two familiar old shoes. Rose's pink lace dress elegantly dusted the gazebo floor, and they danced incessantly.

"Rose, are you OK?"

"I'm fine. Why do you ask?"

"All of the sudden you've gotten so quiet—a little distant."

"I'm just thinking about all of the things that happened to me today."

"Are you sure?"

"Yes, I'm sure. I'm dancing on a cloud that I wish could last forever!"

"You sure are beautiful!"

Rose looked up at him and smiled.

"You're the "Rose" of Benton County," he said giving her a spin around, as they waltzed in the gazebo under the harvest moon.

The band played on...

GAZEBO WALTZ

There you were in the park on that September day.
Just a glance, a chance and we're dancing away.
Our first Hello, how did we know that it would turn out so right?
When we waltzed the gazebo that night!

I held you tight in the light of the harvest moon
Lover's glancing, sweet romancing; it will all end too soon.
I see your eyes, your lovely face, in the misty light,
When we waltzed the gazebo that night.

When I looked to the moon it had turned to gold,
You're the only one my arms will ever hold.
I will never forget how my heart felt delight.
When we waltzed the gazebo that night.

CHAPTER 3: BY THE LIGHT OF THE SILVERY MOON

Sunday was family day. Rose enjoyed going to church. A lot of people gave her big hugs and congratulated her for winning the Sweet Corn Queen title.

Church was just down the road a mile or so. Everyone in the congregation was very close to one another. Most of them were related. Rose's mother, Grace, played the organ on Sundays, and her father, Conrad, sang a deep bass in the choir.

Almost everyone that came to church stayed to enjoy the potluck after the service. Good food and fellowship accompanied many of the church activities that played a big part in the life of this congregation. Grace was well known for contributing her delicious salads. She had a special salad for every occasion. She had a wedding salad, a ladies aid salad, a potluck salad and even a funeral salad. Rose was already doing a good job keeping up with her mother. She brought along a salad of her own that she had made for the potluck. Whether Rose wanted to admit it or not, she was taking after her mother and the other ladies in the church, at least in her cooking skills.

Everyone gathered outside to play games in the churchyard after the potluck was over. Rose participated in the rolling-pin throwing contest. The object of the game was to simply see who could throw it the farthest. Rose eagerly stepped up to throw the pin, and her throw went awry. The rolling pin flew across the crowd and hit someone in the audience. Rose gasped and ran over to see whom it was. It had hit Adam Waterman, the visitor from Baltimore. Rose didn't even know that he was there. He had come to church with Lilly and her family, and they stayed for the potluck.

"Oh no!" Rose shrieked, holding her hand over her mouth. "Are you OK? I'm so sorry! I've always been a bit clumsy," apologized Rose, "but not this clumsy!"

"That's OK," said Mr. Waterman as he gave her a reassuring smile that he would be all right.

"Can I get you some ice to put on it?" offered Rose.

"Sure. That would be great," he agreed, massaging the sore spot on his arm.

Rose quickly made an exit to get some ice. She felt very warm as if she was turning many shades of red. The intensity of her embarrassment grew as she thought about what he must think of her now. With quivering hands, she wrapped ice cubes up in a towel and carried it back to him.

"Thanks, Rose," he said. " I'll be fine. Don't worry about me."

Rose saw to it that he felt better, and then she excused herself. She was so embarrassed that she decided to walk home.

She walked past the apple orchard on the west-side of the road across from the church. Apple Grove got its name from having this beautiful orchard in town. It was located just south of the Railroad Bridge that extended high up into the air. It was only wide enough for one car at a time to drive over. The distinct iron arches on each side of the bridge characterized its uniqueness. It was a well-know bridge in Benton County.

Rose slowly crossed over the bridge and looked out between the arches. She wondered how many times she must have walked over this stately bridge to get to church and to parochial school.

Crossing over this bridge made Rose think of the "crossing over" that she was about to embark on after she had graduated from high school. She wanted to leave her small-town farm-girl image and venture out east to experience city life, far away from family and friends. Could she cross over this bridge successfully or would she have to let go of her dream and stay home and marry safe and steady Wayne?

Rose kept on walking as her mind spun around and around thinking about all kinds of things. She passed through the cemetery, high up on the hill that overlooked the farm.

Down in the green valley below, between the hillside and the farm, there was a pond with two islands in the middle. It was a breathtaking scene with the rolling hills surrounding the pond.

Rose was trying to sort out her feelings. She was beginning to develop a curiosity about this stranger from the east. He was so confident in himself. He was so intriguing. Maybe Wayne wasn't the one for her after all. Maybe it was time that they dated other people for a while before they decided to marry. A lot of uncertainty ran through her mind. Now she found herself questioning everything. Her relationship with Wayne, her own desires, and her future plans for college were in doubt. Rose felt confused about the situation. She struggled to get her thoughts back on track and headed for home, trying to dismiss any impractical thoughts of someone that she would probably never see again. She felt guilty about her thoughts. Her parents liked Wayne, and they would just die if they learned that she was attracted to this easterner!

Rose retreated to her upstairs bedroom to rest. Maybe after a long nap she would have a more clear perspective on things. Usually, after some deep thought over a lengthy period in her room, she could work things out. But this time, things were different. Life seemed to be like red velvet cake batter, all mixed up.

The late afternoon sun was beaming into the south side of the farmhouse. It came in through the ornate stained glass window in the front door like a prism, distributing the rays in a design on the wall by the staircase. Rose came out of her room and sat on the top step admiring the display. The light rays had reflected a beautiful rainbow onto the ceiling. She slowly drifted down the stairway, enjoying the sunshine, as she made her way into the kitchen.

To her surprise, the big, round kitchen table was fully expanded out over its bear-claw legs. It was tastefully decorated with her mother's best white linen tablecloth and matching napkins. It was set with china and silver. These things were their very best.

Grace was busy preparing dinner, consisting of Swiss steak, mashed potatoes and gravy, orange gelatin salad, green-bean casserole, homemade rolls, and rhubarb pie.

Rose began to ask her mother who was coming for dinner when the doorbell rang. She went over to open up the door. In came Adam Waterman. Her stomach took a turn. She tried to greet him as if she knew all along that he was coming.

This is what I get for feeling sorry for myself and hiding out in my room all afternoon, thought Rose.

"I hope that you will forgive me for my clumsiness at the church potluck," apologized Rose. "I was so embarrassed that I just came home."

"No harm done really, and my arm feels fine. I'm just excited to be here for dinner. It was very kind of your mother to invite me over."

"My mother?" Rose asked as she glared at her mother.

"Yes, I think that she felt sorry for me."

"Oh, I see. Well, please, sit down." Rose motioned for him to take a seat.

"This will be a great change from the seafood diet that I'm used to back in Baltimore," said Adam carefully placing his napkin onto his lap.

He still had on a suit. Rose admired his attire and decided that he wore it well. She sat down beside him, eager to carry on more conversation with him.

"What do you do in Maryland?" she asked.

"I'm an investment banker."

"Sounds interesting. And what brings you here?"

"The bank that I work for is interested in investing in Iowa farm land."

"Iowa farm land? Is that really worth investing in right now?"

"The company I work for thinks so."

"So, big eastern investors want to take advantage of our recession and buy up land at low prices. Is that it, Mr. Waterman?" Conrad asked with concern.

Rose could sense that her father was trying to size him up. She wondered if he found him so different from the men around here that he wouldn't like him.

"If I find the right piece of land, Mr. Krueger, I'll pay a fair price for it."

"Lots of farmers are hurting financially right now. Many are selling their farms. It's a sad thing. I'm watching it happen to my friends," added Conrad. "Farms that have been in the family for many years are being sold for a low price. Dreams are being shattered."

"I'm aware of that," agreed Adam. "But I will pay a fair price for the land that I purchase. I wouldn't feel right if I came out here to take advantage of a farm family in the middle of this struggling economy. That's a fact!"

"You sound like a fair man," Conrad said as if he decided to trust Mr. Waterman. "Let's ask a blessing before we begin to eat."

Adam did appear to be a very honest and trustworthy kind of guy. You could see it in his eyes. He had small, deep-set eyes that gleamed as he added a smile. His hair was combed straight back in a sleek and sophisticated manner. His forehead was high, giving him a business-like appearance.

41

Rose decided that it was time to lighten up the topic of conversation, sensing a tense atmosphere surrounding the subject of buying farmland. She knew how concerned her father was about his own financial situation. Rose thought that her father would be devastated if he ever had to sell their family farm. She was brought up thinking that it was never to be sold. It was always to stay in the family, passed down from generation to generation. That's the way she understood it.

"Would you like some more potatoes and gravy, Adam?" asked Rose.

"I'd love some more. Those are the smoothest mashed potatoes that I've ever eaten."

"Adam," Rose interjected, "Where you born and raised in Maryland?"

"Yes, I was born and raised in Baltimore City."

"Right in the heart of the big city?" Rose questioned.

"Right near downtown. I grew up in a row house."

"A row house!" Rose commented surprisingly. "What's that?"

"Adam looked at Rose with shimmering eyes, " It's a row of brick houses that are all attached to one another. They are very common in the big city. More economical, I guess, in such a tight space. It was small, but my parents learned how to make do under the circumstances."

"I bet you got to know your neighbors well," said Grace.

"You're right, Mrs. Krueger. We sure did. We often could hear their conversation through the walls. Especially when someone was upset."

"Where did you go to school?" Asked Rose, who seemed intent on getting to know him better in a short amount of time.

" I went to Green Forrest High and then later went on to Weston College in Chestertown. It's a beautiful and historic university on the Chesapeake Bay that was founded in 1782 or earlier. The early history of the school was lost. It was later raised to the rank of a college and granted a charter by the Maryland assembly."

"It sounds like you really enjoyed going to school there," commented Grace.

"Yes, I sure did, Mrs. Krueger, and I visit the Chesapeake Bay area as often as I can."

"It all sounds so fascinating," smiled Rose.

"Yes, it is. There's so much to see, like the historical sights, the restaurants, and the beautiful scenic trails that follow along the Eastern Shore. One of my favorite things to do is to get a bushel of live crabs and steam them in a big pot. That's a real treat!"

"You actually just put a bunch of live crabs in a pot and eat them?" asked Rose.

"After they're steamed you just pull them apart and peel them for eating. I can sit and do this all evening," said Adam.

"It sounds like a lot of fun!" said Rose. "I'd love to see the bay area. In fact, I'm very interested in attending nursing school out there after I graduate," Rose said giving her father a bold look out of the corner of her eye. "That is if my parents agree."

"St. Mary's has a wonderful nursing school in downtown Baltimore," said Adam. "It's well-known all over the country as one of the top medical institutions. You would definitely get a top education there."

"I want the best for my daughter," Conrad said, " but there is a good school just miles from here where I went to school for awhile before I got called home to help my father farm. I regret never getting the opportunity to finish my schooling. I would like my daughter to have the opportunity to finish. But money is scarce since the depression. We are still trying to figure out how Rose will get her education."

Adam looked down at his plate for a few minutes as if he were in deep thought about something.

Grace noticed that Adam was silent for a long period, so she asked "Is there something wrong with your food?"

"No, Mrs. Krueger, I'm just thinking about something. Maybe I could help!"

"Help who?" inquired Rose.

Adam spoke up with great enthusiasm in his voice. "I came to Iowa to invest in farmland, Mr. Krueger. Is there any part of your land that you would like to sell?"

"Sell my farmland?" Conrad looked at Adam with his mouth wide open.

"This would enable you to finance your daughter's education and I would have accomplished what I have come out here to do."

"No way," Conrad rapidly responded.

"It just sounded like a reasonable suggestion to me, given your situation and mine," Adam explained. "I'm sorry if I upset you Mr. Krueger."

"It's just that I never dreamed that I would sell this farm, let alone have anybody offer me anything for it just out of the blue," Conrad responded.

"You're right. I came up with this idea on the spur of the moment. I'm sorry if I have offended you," Adam apologized again.

"That's all right," said Conrad. "I'd like to give this some more thought."

"That's OK," said Adam. "Forget I brought it up—really."

Just when Rose began to get a little concerned about her father, he spoke out and said, "I might consider selling some of my acres in the back forty. There are a lot of hills back there and I'm getting too old to farm the hills."

Rose felt shockwaves move through her body. She couldn't believe that he was even going to consider this wild and crazy idea. But then her father was a bit of a wheeler-dealer.

"No," Adam quickly answered. "I'm only interested in flat land that has rich, black soil. Land that will hold the value and that I can resell later. Land with a high CSR rating."

"I see you've been doing your homework," said Conrad.

"Well, I had to do a little homework on the subject before I came here."

"My back forty acres have a CSR rating of about 60," Conrad described. "The neighbors to the west might be interested in buying it some day. It has a creek running through it and a nice bunch of trees that could be worth some money. My acres to the east of the farm by the road have a much higher rating. This is some of the best land in Benton County."

"Now we're talking," said Adam. "That's what I'm interested in buying. I'd pay well for that land. Name your price."

Conrad was again taken back by the request. "I would have to give this some thought. That is my best land. Unfortunately, the rest of the farm doesn't fair as well."

"But father," Rose pleaded. "You can't even think about this! You've always said that the farm was to stay in the family."

"I know."

"That's not what you really want to do is it, Conrad?" asked Grace. "You've worked on this farm your entire life and a lot of sweat and tears have gone into it."

"Please, Father, it's supposed to stay in the family," pleaded Rose once again.

Conrad turned to look at Adam and said, "I need some time to think this through."

Rose and her mother, Grace, sighed in unison. They were relieved to see that more thought would be given to this matter.

"That's fine," Adam agreed as he devoured his piece of rhubarb pie enjoying every bite.

Rose looked as if she had the wind knocked out of her. She could not believe the conversation that she was hearing. She had always assumed that the farm would never be sold and that it was to stay in the family. The depression must have been far worse than her father had led her to believe. Rose began to excuse herself from the table.

Noticing her distress, Adam said, "Rose, would you give me a tour around the farm? I'd love to see it. After such a great meal, I could use some fresh air and a walk."

"I guess so," she said as she turned back to look at him.

Rose reluctantly took Adam out to the farmyard for a tour. She really wasn't in the mood to be nice to him at all anymore, but she felt obligated.

The sun had set, and the sky was a beautiful blend of red, orange, and pink.

"It is so peaceful here," remarked Adam.

"Yes it is." answered Rose. I love to listen to the sounds of nature, like the birds chattering, the leaves rustling and the even the cows mooing."

Adam laughed, "I don't consider cows mooing as being very peaceful."

"That's all part of the dairy farm atmosphere," said Rose

"I suppose so," he said. "This is a beautiful place!"

" I do love it here," she said.

"I can see why."

"But the thought of my father selling this land frightens me," Rose admitted.

"Your Father seems like a very intelligent man, Rose. I'm sure that he'll do what he thinks is best."

"You're probably right. He is a wise man!"

Rose continued to show Adam around the farm. She began to feel more at ease with him now. Talking to him helped. He seemed to understand both sides, even though he was the one making the offer. She appreciated his sensitivity to her feelings.

They went inside the corn-crib. Adam admitted that he had never been inside a corn-crib. Rose couldn't believe it. She pulled him into the middle of the crib and told him to just look straight up. It was an ordinary sight taken for granted by Rose, but Adam seemed to just want to stare at the top of the crib for awhile, looking into its vast storage area where many corn cobs stuffed the lining of the exterior walls.

After he was through looking at what seemed a very ordinary sight to Rose, she took him into the chicken house. She told him about how she had raised the chickens and how she had to sell a lot of eggs to get enough money to buy fabric for the Sweet Corn Queen contest. He found that very amusing. He took favor in the rooster that came up close to him and walked around his legs. Rose had used this rooster at the state 4-H convention to promote her ideas while running for state 4-H president. Her slogan was "Something to Crow About."

Rose took him into the machine shed. He seemed to be very interested in seeing the farm equipment up close. He carefully circled around the tractor, inspecting every detail, touching it with his hands.

"What's it feel like to drive this, Rose?"

"I've only had the opportunity once. My father does all of the fieldwork and then he hires other men to help him. The one opportunity that I had was fun, but I'd rather ride my horse."

"Your horse? Where do you keep it?"

"In the barn. I'll show you."

Located on the north side of farm, was the massive dairy barn. It bore the name, **CONRAD KRUEGER** on the top in big, bold letters.

"Wow, that's a big barn, Rose!"

"It sure is. I have all kinds of secret hiding places inside.

"Show me one."

"Can you climb a ladder?" Rose teased.

"Why sure I can. My father was a carpenter."

"But you have on a nice suit?"

"It'll clean."

"OK—follow me," she said.

Rose led him inside the barn. To the left of the entryway there was a wooden ladder extending up into the loft. Rose climbed up the ladder so quickly that she left Adam in the dust.

"Are you coming?" Rose shouted down the opening in the loft to the first floor.

"I'm on my way," he answered.

Adam reached the top and stood up to take in the view.

"Wow! This is immense!"

"Over here is one of my hideouts that I had as a child," Rose pointed out. "I used to love to play up here."

"I can see why. This is incredible!"

They walked around the top floor of the barn and looked out all of the windows from each direction. This was really a good way to get a look at the land that surrounded the farm. Adam studied it carefully.

"Your folks keep this place looking very neat and tidy," Adam commented.

"Yes, they do. Many people have told us that it is one of the sharpest looking farms around."

"I can believe that."

"Are you ready to climb back down, Adam? You're getting hay all over your nice suit."

"I guess you're right," he said brushing the hay off of his pants and his jacket. "Show me your horse."

"He's out in the pasture. Let's go out and I'll call for him," said Rose.

They walked out to the east of the barn. Rose whistled for the horse to come.

"Buck, come here boy!" she called.

"With a name like that I'm not sure that I'd get on him," Adam commented.

"Oh, it doesn't mean anything, really. He's very gentle."

Buck came right up to Rose, and they both began to pet his mane.

"He's very nice," said Adam.

"Want to ride him?"

"Sure!"

"I was just kidding. You have your suit on."

"That's OK. I'll try it."

"I'll get a bridle," said Rose as she walked toward the barn.

She came back out of the barn shaking her head in disbelief that he was really going to get on Buck in his suit. She slipped the bit in the horse's mouth as if there was nothing to it.

"OK. He's all yours cowboy!" she teased.

Adam jumped up and lifted a leg right over, mounting faster than Rose imagined, and with ease. Adam gave a slight kick and off he went, out to the pasture for the ride of his life! Buck must have known that he was an inexperienced rider. He took off faster than he'd ever taken off before. Rose became frightened and called for him to come back to the barn, giving him instructions on how to handle Buck. He got Buck turned back in the direction of the barn and they came flying down the lane. The look on Adam's face was a sight to behold. Neither Adam nor Rose was sure what Buck was going to do next. But it didn't take long, and they knew. Buck came running toward the barn as if he was going to throw Adam off onto the cement when he stopped abruptly just shy of the barn door. Rose ran over to help him get off.

Adam climbed down with a big smile on his face and said, "Not bad for a city boy, right?"

"I've had enough excitement for one day, Adam! You had me very worried there for awhile," Rose said as she took the bridle off of Buck and let him go. "Let's go sit awhile on the porch swing. I think that you've seen everything now."

"The sun is beginning to go down," Adam observed. "That sounds like a good idea."

They sat on the porch enjoying the rest of the evening until the moon became full and bright. It radiated above them in the calm night sky. The chirping sounds of the night insects began to accompany their conversation.

"Oh—Rose, this is the life! You're so lucky! This is a great place to have grown up. It's so much better than the cramped, busy life of the city. It's quiet and peaceful here—simple—relaxing. You don't have all the hustle and bustle of city life. You have more freedom. I would love living here."

"You would? I'm just the opposite. I would trade you in a minute. I'm tired of being on the farm. I'm ready to get out in the world—to experience more of what life has to offer."

"I can understand where you are coming from. You're young and ready to test your own wings. I've done a little of that, being a few years older than you are. Once you get away, you'll appreciate what you have here a whole lot more."

"Maybe you're right, but now I'm ready to go. What do you like best about living in Baltimore?"

"I really like the *wooder*. I love the ocean and watching the tide roll in at sunset. I grew up going to the ocean for vacations. My folks liked to get a room on the boardwalk and spend lots of time on the beach.

"I also like the bay area and looking at all the big ships in the shipyard. I guess that would be one thing that I might miss if I lived out here in the Mid-West."

"We have lakes. You'd just have to get yourself a boat and a cabin on a nearby lake. You could still enjoy the water."

"This is true. I could learn to *wooder* ski."

"I like your accent."

"My accent? I didn't know I had one. You're the one with the accent."

"I've just noticed your accent on a few of your words, especially the way you say water."

"You mean *wooder*," Adam retorted.

"No, I mean water," she said.

"Are you teasing me, Rose?"

"Maybe just a little," she giggled.

They both enjoyed visiting long into the evening. Rose became swept up in the moment, indulging in conversation about what it would be like to go east and fulfill her dream of becoming a nurse. She temporarily forgot about the present, and Wayne Johnson!

CHAPTER 4.: RED ROSES FOR A BLUE LADY

The next morning Rose over-slept. She woke up, quickly got dressed, and rushed down stairs to talk to her father.

"Father, what did you decide to do about Mr. Waterman's offer to buy some land?"

"Rose, please sit down. I need to talk to you about my decision," said her father.

Rose took a seat, anxious to hear him out, hoping for the best.

"I have decided to sell the farm to Mr. Waterman," he firmly stated.

"The entire farm?" Rose squealed.

"No, not the entire farm. Just the land."

"How much land?"

"All two hundred and fifty acres."

"What about our house?"

" I want to keep the house and the building sights that are on the five acres that surround it."

"Why? Why?" Rose pleaded.

"Rose, the depression has been very hard on us. Mr. Waterman has made us a very generous offer that we may never see again in our lifetimes!"

"Have you discussed this with Mother?"

"Yes, we have discussed this in great length, and I have been up all night thinking about it. I really think that this is the right thing to do at this time."

"But Father," cried Rose. "You can't sell the land now! It is supposed to stay in the family."

"Sometimes we have to do what we have to do in a given situation to survive, Rose," said her father. "This decision just might spare the next generation the burden of deciding what to do with the farm. That burden could cause a lot of problems for the family members that are involved."

"What do you mean, Father?"

What if the farm were left to a generation of children or grandchildren that could not agree with each other? I don't want to be held responsible for breaking apart future generations. Mr. Waterman just might be the answer."

"But... "

"Rose," her father interrupted, " I have already made the deal with Mr. Waterman early this morning. He's already on his way back to Baltimore."

"What? You've already made the deal this morning before I even got up?" Rose sobbed as she tried to comprehend all that her father was telling her. "I didn't even get a chance to say goodbye!"

Rose got up from her chair, and she whisked out the back door. She was very upset with her father, and she needed to sort out her feelings. She needed time to think this through.

Rose walked down the gravel road into town. She found this quite helpful on occasion when she needed to work out some problem in her life.

She loved walking into town. Everyone was so cordial. Rose especially liked to visit with the owners of the general store when she stopped to pick up the mail occasionally. A small section in the store was the post office.

The general store was a neat little place to go. They carried just about everything in that store from dry goods to high button shoes. It was a beautiful store with solid oak cabinets. The corners of the cabinets had a smooth rounded look for a warm and welcoming atmosphere.

The Smith's owned the general store. Mr. and Mrs. Smith were very nice people and they loved to visit with Rose whenever she came in.

Mrs. Smith was a short, plump little lady with a round, friendly face. Her salt and pepper hair was combed back into a bun that she placed high on top of her head. She always wore an apron.

The children in the town liked going there after school. It was amazing how much candy one could buy for a penny! She patiently stood behind the counter everyday with a warm smile and assisted the often long tedious task of children selecting their candy. She would carefully place each treasured piece in a special little brown paper bag that was just the right size.

Mr. Smith was just as short and just as plump as his wife was. He also had an amicable smile, but his hair had a lot more gray in it than Mrs. Smith's did. In fact, it was almost all white with lots of soft waves across the back. The young children in the town had nicknamed them Mr. and Mrs. Santa Claus.

As Rose was walking up the step to pull open the door to the General Store, she noticed a rather large poster hanging up to the left of the front door. It had a picture of a glamorous blonde woman all dressed up in overalls and a bandanna with her sleeves rolled up. It looked like a real symbol of patriotic womanhood, as she saluted. It said, "WANTED - FEMALE HELP," calling for production workers, sales clerks, kitchen help and housekeepers. It also said, "WOMEN URGENTLY NEEDED BY U.S. FOR STENO WORK." Apply at the courthouse in Cedar City.

Rose wondered what this was all about. It looked to her like the women were badly needed. Rose opened up the door and went inside.

"How are you today, Rose?" asked Mr. Smith.

"Oh, I'm fine, I guess," said Rose as she tried to look like she was happy, but the truth began to show as she hesitated to speak. "I guess I haven't had very good news this morning. In fact, I've had some very bad news this morning," she said as tears began to descend down her cheeks.

"What's wrong dear?" Mrs. Smith asked in a soft and concerned voice.

Rose was always a happy girl. They had never seen her like this.

"My father just sold the farm this morning. I'm really startled by his decision," said Rose. "It seems so unreasonable. I shouldn't even be speaking to you about this, but I'm just so flustered. I thought I'd come in town for a walk and hopefully feel better."

"Oh, we're sorry, Rose," said Mrs. Smith. "I hope that your father made the right decision."

"Your father is a very smart man, Rose," added Mr. Smith. "I'm sure he did the right thing."

"Here, Rose," offered Mrs. Smith. "Have an ice cream on us. This should make you feel better!"

Mr. and Mrs. Smith had very warm hearts, and even though times were tough, they often shared with others.

Rose loved their ice cream. It was a very rich ice cream with a smooth texture. They would take a big scoop of ice cream on a stick and dip it in rich chocolate and freeze it until it was ice cold.

"Thanks," said Rose. "This is my favorite ice cream. I appreciate your kindness and your listening to me. I'll be OK. I just need some time to get used to the idea. Say, what's that poster all about on your front door?"

"It looks like the country is gearing up to get heavily involved in the war. Women will be needed urgently to hold down the home front in as many ways as possible. Things are going to be changing really quickly for our country now, Rose. We will all have to get involved and do our part, even us small town folks here in Apple Grove."

"How do you think things will change, Mr. Smith?"

"Americans are now being urged to change their way of thinking," he said.

"For example the new motto is to Use it Up, Wear it Out, Make it Do or Do Without!"

"But we are already accustomed to thinking that way from experiencing the depression," she noted.

"Yes, but now we will experience shortages in different areas, such as gasoline, rubber, sugar, butter and meat."

"Why those shortages?" Rose wondered.

Mrs. Smith reminded Rose, "Because these things will be going to the troops. There already is a shortage of sugar. Why just the other day a couple stopped in to buy a wedding present and they bought 2 pounds of sugar."

"Two pounds of sugar for a wedding present?" asked Rose.

"It's back to the basics now!" Mrs. Smith affirmed.

"Why I guess so," agreed Rose. "But how can everyone get involved?"

"Boys and girls can collect used tin cans, old tires and other things that could be recycled and used for war supplies," explained Mr. Smith. Some of our nation's women will have to enlist in the armed forces and others will have to stay on the home front and work in the manufacturing plants in the cities."

Rose seemed surprised to hear that women would need to roll up their sleeves and work in very masculine roles. "What kind of manufacturing plants would be hiring women?"

"Defense plants, packing plants, and even the big tractor plants up north are doing their best to aid in the war effort. Women will be filling important places in society to fill the vacancies that will be left by the men who will fight for our country."

"Do you have any idea how much money one can make on the production line?"

"I've heard from the grapevine that it's about fifty cents per hour. Women will be asked to work in heavy and tedious jobs in hot and humid environments," answered Mrs. Smith.

"Sounds to me like women will have to become Wonder Women," Rose commented.

"I think you're right, Rose. But there is something that all of us can do. We can give our soldiers morale support by sending them letters and gift packages now and then," Mrs. Smith suggested.

"That's a good idea, Mrs. Smith. Even I could do that. I can't imagine myself working on a production line after I graduate, but I could write letters. I still would like to go out east for school, but I'm not sure if I'll be able to yet. We don't have it all worked out."

"Rose, you've always been a bright gal. I'm sure you'll have a bright future. Your folks are fine people. I'm sure that they will see to it that you do," Mrs. Smith said zealously.

"Rose, there is also another way that you and your family can get involved in the war effort," suggested Mr. Smith. "Farm families are being urged to increase food production at home."

"In what way?"

"You could plant a victory garden in your own back yard," proposed Mrs. Smith. "If more Americans could grow more for themselves, more food and supplies could be sent overseas."

"What should we plant in our victory garden?"

Mr. smith advised, "Peas, carrots, corn and tomatoes would be a good start. You can save the seeds for the following year."

"I'll share this with my family," Rose resolved. "It would be a great way for our family to be involved together. Thanks for sharing all of this information with me today. You two are swell!"

"Any time, Rose. Say, there's going to be a band concert here tonight. You and your parents might be interested in coming in for it. We're going to pull in a hayrack for the band to play on and there will be dancing in the street. It should be fun. Bring your folks along. It would be good for your family to enjoy the evening," suggested Mr. Smith.

"I'll tell them. Sounds like a good idea. Thanks again for the ice cream and maybe we'll be back tonight."

Rose journeyed back out to the farm, enjoying every bit of her ice cream on a stick. It seemed to pick up her spirits as she walked along the familiar road from downtown Apple Grove to her farmhouse.

Rose was able to persuade her parents into going to town that evening for the band concert. Grace agreed that it was a good idea to help lift their spirits.

Downtown Apple Grove was a bustling little town. When you first came into town, there was a gas station and a garage. Conrad went there often to visit with his friends and to have coffee. And along with the coffee came the local news spread by word of mouth sweetened with sugar cubes.

To the north of the garage was a blacksmith shop. This was also a place where the men would gather on occasion to have their morning coffee.

Across the street to the east were the main-street businesses. First, there was a corner grocery store, and then next to it was the General Store that Mr. and Mrs. Smith owned. Next came a tavern that very often had a white horse tied up to a hitching post out in front of it. It belonged to a regular customer and a long time resident of Apple Grove. After school, a few kids would wander by the tavern from the public school and jump right up to sit on the horse for a while. Lots of miles were traveled on that old white horse or one should say pretend miles. The merchants didn't seem to care. They just figured that it was keeping those boys busy instead of picking fights with the Lutheran school-boys.

Then came the second general store that had a separate room off of it just to store flour in. The bank followed on main-street. Rumors were circulating that the bank was about to close. Across the street was a grain elevator that just recently survived a frightening explosion in the middle of the night when someone blew up the safe and got away with a large sum of money. Next to the grain elevator was the lumberyard where farmers went to buy their fence posts.

It was a beautiful evening and it seemed like everyone in town came to listen to the band. They played on top of the hayrack in the middle of Main Street. They played songs like *Back Beat Boogie, Scatterbrain, I'll Be Seeing You,* and *Deep Purple.* People strolled up and down the street drinking rootbeer, and children were going in and out of the general store buying the fancy ice cream on a stick.

Some began to dance in the street around the hayrack. They were doing a dance called the Jitterbug. Everyone was having a great time together until all of the sudden someone let out a loud scream! It came from the east, down the road past main-street. People began to quickly make their way into the general stores and the tavern.

Something was beginning to frighten the town people. Something was about to happen.

Conrad took Rose and her mother by the hand and said, "Come on let's go into Smith's store, hurry!"

They immediately followed orders and quickly crowded into the store. The store was full of people, and Mr. Smith locked the front door to the street.

The store became quiet and Rose heard a faint whisper in the far distant end of the store. "Are the Gypsies gone yet, Mama?"

CHAPTER 5: IN THE GOOD OLD SUMMERTIME

The days to follow were very busy for Rose and her family. Conrad continued to farm the land owned by the bank in Baltimore on a sharecrop basis.

Rose never quite fully accepted the fact that her father sold all of their land. She still felt a deep sense of loss. She wondered if her father felt the same way, but she felt uneasy talking about it.

The last year of high school went by quickly for Rose and was occupied with many activities. She continued to date Wayne, participated in 4-H, church activities and school functions. Her relationship with Wayne became increasingly stronger, and Rose forgot about any feelings that she had felt during her brief acquaintance with Adam Waterman, the eastern investor. She was angry with him for leaving so abruptly, and it was true that out of sight became out of mind.

⊰⊱⊰⊱⊰⊱

It was May of 1942. Rose was graduating from high school. She thought that this day would never arrive.

The graduation ceremony was held in the high school gym. It was a hot afternoon, and the gymnasium filled up with people sitting in chairs and standing all around the edges. There was standing room only. Everyone must have invited a lot of relatives. The air became thick and the room stuffy. People were making fans out of their programs to get some air circulating around their faces. An elderly lady fainted right in the front row just before the program had started.

The graduates made their way through the thick crowd of people from the back of the gymnasium to the tune of the traditional graduation march. Sweat was beading down many of their foreheads from underneath their black mortarboard hats with the long tassel off to one side.

It became time for Rose to come down the aisle. She was able to pair up with Wayne. They both looked very hot and sticky, but they had big smiles on their faces showing that they were truly happy to be taking this final step forward into the future.

Grace and Conrad sat near the front, beaming with pride to see their daughter graduating from high school. Grace was wondering if she would see Rose and Wayne walking down another aisle together in the near future. She secretly hoped so.

As the Class President, Rose was given the honor of presenting the class of 1942 with the graduation speech. She talked about all of the good memories that they had shared together as a class. She also encouraged everyone to reach for his or her dreams and to never give up. She challenged them to be all that they could be and to diligently strive to accomplish their goals. She closed the speech wishing each and every one of them lots of luck and good fortune followed by the invocation. The audience was captivated by her presentation, and it drew a standing burst of applause.

As they walked down the aisle, Wayne looked at Rose and he said, "I hope that this isn't the last time that we walk down the aisle together."

Rose looked back at him with bright eyes, curving the corners of her mouth upward.

After the grand ceremony of graduation was over at the high school, many people were invited to the farm for a hog roast. It had taken Grace weeks to plan this party, and she was looking a bit jaded. She was busy making the final preparations for the arrival of many guests, to include all of the cousins and church friends. Frantically, she was trying to thaw out the coleslaw.

The class colors were red, white, and blue, and the class flower was the red rose. Grace decorated with red, white, and blue streamers and balloons. The sheet cakes were topped with red roses. Mints were attractively displayed on plates that were made in the shape of red roses and green leaves. Grace and Rose had worked for several days before to carefully mold and shape each delicate mint out of a cream cheese and sugar mixture.

Conrad was setting up the chairs and tables in the yard. The sky looked bright and sunny. The weather was definitely cooperating today. There wasn't a cloud in the sky.

On the east-side of the farmyard there was a stage being set up by a few talented neighbors that were going to play some music for the occasion on a variety of stringed instruments. They were setting up around the corn-crib which Conrad and the hired man had worked so hard to clean up the day before. Inside the corn-crib, tables were set up to hold the food.

Rose was still up in her room trying to decide what to change into for the party. She was rummaging through the bottom of her closet, looking for just the right pair of bobby socks. It was fashionable for your legs to look like tree trunks. All the girls scrunched thick bobby socks around their ankles. It was the thing to do. Rose was looking for just the right pair. She had an entire wardrobe of bobby socks. Some she had knitted herself in an argyle plaid. Some had her initials on them. Her favorite pair, the checkerboard ones, seemed to be missing for the party. She searched under the last pile in the back of her closet and then uncovered the right pair. She quickly pulled them out and put them on with a pair of scuffed saddle shoes.

She finished getting ready and turned to glance out the window. Cars were coming down the driveway. Wayne was the first one, followed by her classmates, and then some cousins. Rose couldn't wait to see them. She barreled downstairs and out the back door to the yard waving at her guests.

Grace had finished setting up the food tables and people were streaming in. The yard quickly filled with people laughing, dancing, and celebrating this special day with Rose.

Wayne found Rose in the crowd and asked, "Would you like to dance?"

"Sure," said Rose.

As they walked over to the dance area, Wayne took her hand and said, "Rose, congratulations! I'm glad we made it! Have you decided what you are going to do?"

She turned to him and placed her arm on his shoulder as they embraced for a close dance. "Not just yet. How about you?"

"My plans haven't changed. I'm still going to stay here and farm with my father unless I get drafted now that we are going to war. Then I'd have to serve my country for awhile until the war gets over and I could come back to help my father."

"I hope that it works out for you the way you want it to."

"Can I tempt you to stay here in Apple Grove and marry me?"

Rose stopped dancing and looked up into his eyes. "Is this a proposal Wayne Johnson?"

"I—I guess so," he stuttered as if he had surprised himself as well.

She looked down at the ground for a moment in deep thought pausing before answering him. "No. I can't just yet."

"What do you mean you can't just yet? Your plans are still up in the air. You could make up your mind today, right now at this very moment!"

"Wayne, we've gone over this before."

"I know, but that was some time ago. A lot has happened since the last time we discussed it."

"Like what?"

"Well, for one thing, we've graduated."

"And?"

"We've both grown up."

"Grown up? It was just last summer when we talked about this, when you gave me your class ring," she reminded him.

"Yes, and you said that you would take it, then. Now the time has come. I need to know, Rose. Do we have a future? I need some answers."

"I don't know yet. I'm still going to go to school, one way or another. You just wait and see. I will. It'll be worked out soon. Let's talk about something else. Suddenly I feel weak."

Wayne pressed further, "I don't want to talk about something else. I want an answer right now!"

Rose backed her body away from his and looked him straight in the eye, "If you want to marry me, you'll have to wait!" She turned away and hotfooted into the house.

Rose didn't sulk too long. After all, it was her graduation day, and she didn't want to upset her guests or her parents. Determined not to ruin her special day, she resolved her frustrations and went back out to join the festivities. She looked around for Wayne. It appeared that he had left.

The party wound down shortly after dark, and all-in-all, it was regarded as a huge success. Grace and Conrad were pleased, but Rose felt badly about what had happened between Wayne and her.

After a restless night's sleep, from all of the excitement of graduation, Rose picked up the phone to give Wayne a call just as soon as she had gotten up. She was feeling a little guilty about the way that she had spoken to him at the party.

"Wayne?"

"Hello, Rose."

"I'm sorry. I've been thinking about it all night. I spoke too harshly."

"No, that's alright. I deserved it. I was pushing. Forget it. Take your time. I'm not going anywhere."

"Thanks, Wayne."

"For what?"

"For being patient and understanding."

"I have a feeling I'm going to have to be a lot more patient and understanding in the future."

"Maybe not."

"Oh, I think so. You're quite a gal with lots of dreams."

"I guess so."

"But that's fine, Rose. Get them all out of your system and them come back to me. I'll wait."

"Are you sure?"

"Yes, I'm sure."

"I'll talk to you later, Wayne."

"OK."

"Rose, who was that on the telephone?" her mother called from the kitchen. "Come join your father and I for breakfast."

"Oh, it was just Wayne," she answered. "I had some apologizing to do."

"Did you and Wayne have a falling out last night?" asked her father. "I saw him leave the party in a hurry, not saying good-bye to anyone. That is not like him."

"Is everything OK between you and Wayne?" asked her mother.

Rose took a seat at the breakfast table a little hesitant to share what had happened between Wayne and her last night. She knew that her parents really liked Wayne and hoped that she would stay close to home now and decide to marry him. Bringing up the fact that he proposed to her last night might only hurt her chances of getting to go out east to school. She took a moment to collect her thoughts before speaking to her parents about it.

"I guess it's time that we come to some decisions about my future," said Rose. "I can't put it off any longer. Last night Wayne asked me to marry him."

"Oh Rose, that's wonderful!" cried her mother.

"That's just perfect!" her father interjected.

"It is not perfect!" Rose firmly objected. "That's not at all what I want to do right now. I'm not saying that I will never marry Wayne Johnson, but I do know that I'm certainly not ready right now!"

"But Rose, Wayne really loves you. He always has," her mother stated.

"I know, Mother, but I don't know if I really love him. I've always known how you and Father have felt about him, but as for me, well

I'm not at all certain how I feel. I'm too young to get married just yet. I'm still changing just like this country is changing. The war is picking up speed throughout the country and I want to do my part for the war effort."

"That's true," her father agreed. "Everyone does seem to be pitching in."

"Yes, and I want to get involved too," she said.

"Have you been reading the newspaper lately?" asked her father.

"No, I've been so busy with graduation and all that I haven't looked at it for awhile."

"They are advertising to attract women to go into the Cadet Nursing Corps," said her father.

Upon hearing this Rose became very intrigued.

"Father, I'd like to get more information about joining."

"I think that we could find out more about this in Cedar City at the courthouse. I'd be glad to take you there," he said.

"Great! Let's go tomorrow," said Rose.

"Are you sure that this is the something that you really want to look into?" asked her mother.

"Yes, I'm positive, Mother."

"You are very strong-willed," said her father.

Conrad paused for a moment and then looked at Grace.

"Grace, its time for us to let go and let her make her own decisions."

Her parents agreed. It was time to let their daughter grow up. They took the train into the city the very next day.

When they arrived at the courthouse, they discovered that Rose could be trained to be a cadet nurse at the finest nursing school in the country. They were offering this program at St. Mary's in Baltimore, Maryland. This was the very same nursing school that Adam Waterman had told them about the night that they had him over for dinner. Some of the tuition would be wavered in exchange for service in the Corps.

" Rose," said her father, " I have enough money from the sale of the farm to pay for the remaining amount that the Corps won't pay for to get you to this school in the east. Is this what you still want to do?"

"Yes! Absolutely!" she confirmed.

"It looks like your dream is finally about to come true!" said her father.

Rose could hardly believe what she was hearing. She had waited and hoped for so long to hear these words from her father's mouth.

"Thank you so much!" Rose said as she gave her father a hug. "When can I go?"

CHAPTER 6: TILL WE MEET AGAIN

The brick floor on the depot landing was a faded orange that matched the leaves on the trees.

"Wayne, I promise, I'll write to you as often as I can. In fact, I'll write every day," said Rose. "I don't want to leave, but this is the opportunity that I've been hoping for. You do understand don't you?"

"Yes, I understand," answered Wayne still looking a bit long-faced. But I'll be looking forward to seeing you again during the holidays. I hope the time passes quickly. I'll try to keep busy during the fall harvest, and then before you know it, you'll be home for Christmas!"

Rose tearfully said goodbye to Wayne and her parents.

"We love you Rose," her father yelled as he watched his only daughter board the train headed for Baltimore.

Saying goodbye was more difficult than they had imagined.

Rose had begun the journey of her dreams. As she stepped on board, the conductor greeted her with an affectionate smile. She walked down through the aisle looking for just the right seat. Rose was surprised to find such roomy, comfortable coach seats that you could stretch out on. A window seat near the middle of the coach looked the most inviting. Swinging her tote bag around to her lap, she pulled out a good book, thinking that the trip might get a little long.

As the train began to pull away from the train station, Rose waved out the window at Wayne and her folks. They were still there waiting to see her off. Her mother was blowing kisses, one right after the other. She felt a deep vacancy in her stomach. There were so many unknowns ahead of her. She wondered what it would be like. *Will I make it on my own?*

The train began to pick up speed. She could no longer see her family. She noticed the panoramic view from the train. The landscape was beautiful.

What a way to see the countryside, she thought. The train was even smoother and more placid than she imagined in would be. Rose was traveling in the economy class, but she was surprised at how many special features that were on board the train. Not only were the seats reclining, they had fold-down trays and over-head reading lights. They included leg rests and pillows for over-night travel.

Rose began making preparations to spend the night on the train. She chose to sleep in her seat that reclined. It was much cheaper than getting a private sleeping car. Those were only for people traveling in the first-class section. They were equipped with private sleeping accommodations with comfortable beds, special services, and larger windows for a private view of the countryside.

The train also had a dining car. A full range of snacks, sandwiches, and beverages were available to purchase at lunch. Dinner was featured with sit-down dining with white linen table clothes and china. On long distance trips, the dining car was the social center of the train. You could purchase a snack and still enjoy the view. The dining car was open to all passengers, but the meals were included in the ticket price for the sleeping car passengers. Rose just felt fortunate to be able to take the train to Baltimore. She didn't mind that she was traveling the most economical way.

Rose couldn't wait to go through Pennsylvania to get a glimpse of the mountain scenery and the spectacular fall foliage. She had heard about the long tunnels that went right through the mountains and wondered what it would be like to go through them. She was hoping that she wouldn't be asleep when they made their way through the Dutch countryside.

Philadelphia was another place on the route that she had heard so much about. Maybe from the train she would get to see the Philadelphia Museum of Art and the College Boathouse along the

Schuylkill River. Philadelphia was full of history and culture, which Rose was hoping to get a feel for, even through the window of the train.

Then would come the nation's capitol. She hoped to see the stunning monuments and the fantastic city-scape that she had only studied about in high school. The train route was supposed to follow the actual route of the B&O Railroad, viewing the beautiful Potomac River Valley to the Allegheny Mountains.

✑✑✑

After two days on the train, Rose arrived to her destination in Baltimore, Maryland. The trip went well and Rose got to see lots of countryside with very little sleep. She had stayed up most of the night because she was so exhilarated about the trip.

The train depot in downtown Baltimore looked very different than the one that she had left from in Cedar City. She collected her luggage and found a cab to take her over to St. Mary's.

Rose arrived at the nursing school without any problems. The school had mailed her good directions. She found the registration office and met a guide that had been assigned to her upon arrival. She registered, and her guide took her to the dormitory area that was just to the north of the hospital. Rose was very anxious to meet her new roommate.

Rose arrived to a busy first week of orientation activities planned by the nursing school. She could hardly believe that she was finally in Maryland. It was breathtaking. She didn't have time to feel homesick.

She really liked her roommate, Betty. She was from Baltimore City. They hit it off immediately. Betty liked a lot of the same things that Rose did. They shared many similar interests.

Betty was from the city, but she had very high values, and she liked adventure like Rose. She was a kind and caring person, which seemed to go well with the personality of a nurse. Betty liked to care

69

for people, and she began to look out for Rose since she was so far from home and her family. They bonded from the very day that they met, and their friendship grew into a long and lasting one.

Every morning Rose rushed down to the mailboxes to see if she had gotten a letter from home. Wayne sent her a letter every day. Her parents sent a letter once a week. She enjoyed writing back to them and sharing her new experiences in great detail.

The letters from Wayne were quite amusing. He seemed to really miss Rose. Rose hoped that he would get used to her being gone pretty soon or at least find another hobby.

The letters from her parents gave her strength and a quiet peace about being so far from home. She knew that they had missed her too, but they didn't go on about it in their letters like Wayne did. They didn't want to make her homesick.

This day's letter from Wayne was different. It carried a new tone.

Dear Rose,

Guess what? Something has happened that I never thought would happen to me. I've been called to serve my country! I've been drafted into the army. I'm scheduled to leave very soon. I guess that my father will have to make it without me for a while. He seems to be worried. I hope that the war doesn't last very long and that I can return home soon. Remember Rose—I will always love you!

Till we meet again,
Wayne

As Rose read this letter she wept for Wayne. She knew that this was not what he wanted to do. The only thing that he ever wanted to do was to farm with his father. Now this would interrupt his life, but she wasn't sure as to what degree.

At first the soldiers were volunteer only, but now the war department was beginning to draft men of all different backgrounds, not giving them any say in the matter. The country needed more men to fight. Everyone was being called upon to serve in some capacity or another.

"Betty, I just got a letter from Wayne back home. He's been drafted into the Army and I'm terrified for him," said Rose. "He's not the fighting type! What if something happens to him and I never see him again? What then?"

Betty sat down near Rose ready to listen. She was good at doing this when Rose was upset, and she always knew just what to say in response to her concerns.

"Rose, I can understand how you are feeling. Many men that are being drafted into service are scared to death of going. This war is an awful thing and it's affecting all of our lives right now. We need good men like Wayne to help us end this war. Try to see the purpose of it all."

"It's just that I never thought that someone I loved would be called to serve from back home," said Rose.

"I know," said Betty. "These are hard times for many people, Rose. Lot's of women have to say goodbye to their sweethearts, wondering if they will ever see them again. Some will and some won't. That's a fact of this cold war. Try to be positive for Wayne's sake."

"You're right, Betty. I'll be strong for him. Thanks for being here for me and being such a great friend!" said Rose.

Wayne was not the only one that was being called to serve. Many men and women across America found themselves having to suddenly answer their country's call to a higher degree than ever before. Fifteen million young people served in the armed forces, and those who could not serve found other means to help the morale of the troops and those that were back home.

The government established the United Service Organization (USO) to bolster the morale of the American troops. This project was financed by the American people and not by government funds.

The Army and the Navy directed it. They constructed three hundred USO facilities in various locations around the country. Shows for draftees began emerging all over the country.

Rose noticed a large poster placed on the bulletin board in the hallway of her dormitory. It was announcing the first USO show that was coming soon to the Naval base in Annapolis. St. Mary's nursing students were invited to participate in the USO Queen Pageant. Student nurses were invited to help join the war effort and to help boost the morale of the troops. Rose decided to talk this over with her roommate Betty, who so graciously listened to her affairs.

"Betty," asked Rose, "did you see the poster on the bulletin board in the hallway about running for USO queen?"

"Yes, I did and I thought of you."

"Me?"

"Yes, you have experience being in a pageant back home. I think that you should try again," encouraged Betty.

"I guess I do. It might be a good way for me to get involved in the war effort."

"Yes, and you would be good at it. You would meet a lot of girls from all over the country and best of all, a lot of available GIs!"

Rose chuckled, "Maybe you should do it too, Betty."

"No thanks. I'll leave the beauty pageants to you!"

"I think I'll do it. It sounds fun!"

"Good for you, Rose!"

"Thanks for the encouragement," said Rose. "What kind of gown do you think that I should wear?"

"Gee, I don't know, Rose. You have very good taste. You'd be better at selecting that than I."

"I was thinking about a gown made out of a satin fabric in a soft pastel color," said Rose.

"Yes, and maybe off-the-shoulder. Something very elegant," suggested Betty.

"Do you think that I should add a head piece?" asked Rose.

"Maybe something simple that would compliment the gown."

"See, Betty, you know more about this after all."

"I guess maybe I do. It's fun to help plan your outfit."

"Are you sure that you don't want to participate in the pageant yourself?"

"I'm sure, Rose. But I'll come watch you."

"That would be great! I could use someone there to cheer for me."

Rose began to make preparations for the contest in a similar manner to which she had planned back in Iowa for the Sweet Corn Festival. She found it much easier to plan this time, but this competition was on a much larger scale. There would be a lot of beautiful girls from all over. Nevertheless, Rose accepted the challenge with even greater confidence than ever before.

Getting involved in as many activities as she could, kept her from thinking about how much she missed Wayne. She found herself all wrapped up in the events leading up to the USO show until the day had arrived for her to go.

෯෯෯

There were about 50 nursing students that were participating in the contest. They chartered a bus from the school to the Naval base for the weekend event. It was late in September, almost one year from when she had won the Sweet Corn Queen contest back in Benton County, Iowa. Here she was again traveling to be in another contest.

Rose found the trip to the capitol of Maryland to be exquisite. Annapolis was not too far from Baltimore, and she thought that it lived up to its name, America's sailing capitol. The past and the present were reflected in all areas of the community. Rose especially enjoyed the stylish boutiques, the quaint restaurants, and the historical, colonial atmosphere.

After a tour around Annapolis, the bus arrived down at the pier of the Naval base. The nurses got out of the bus to find a breathtaking scene. There were flat bed trucks holding twenty-four-foot mobile stages on top. Each stage had a piano, floodlights, and microphones.

It was an open-air, stand-up-and-watch-it theater all surrounded in the background with huge Navy ships by the docks.

The USO had arranged an escort for each nursing student to help them get around for the weekend. Rose was anxious to meet hers.

One by one the escorts came up to the girls as they called out their names. All of the men were officers dressed up in their uniforms. These guys were very handsome, and big smiles and giggles circulated throughout the group of nursing students.

"Greetings Miss Krueger. We meet again!"

The voice sounded familiar to Rose as she turned to meet the approaching officer. The sun was shining in such a way that she couldn't quite see his face. Rose held her hand over her brow to shade the sunlight. Rose looked again with anticipation to see who was greeting her. The voice sounded a little like Adam Waterman's.

"Adam, is that you?" Rose asked with curiosity in her voice.

"Yes, Rose, it's me."

"What a surprise to see you! What are you doing here?"

"I enlisted in the Navy as an officer."

"An officer?"

"Yes, and I see you made it out here for nurses training after all."

"Finally!" she smiled.

"It also looks as if you are running for another title."

"Yes," she chuckled. " I entered this contest to contribute to the war effort in my own way. I guess this is an area that I have a little experience in."

" I remember well. How could I forget a face like yours? Come this way and I'll show you where you can get ready for the show," said Adam as he extended his arm out for her to hold onto. "This should be a fabulous event!"

Rose hesitated to accept his arm. She still felt angry toward him for leaving Iowa without even saying good-bye to her. She wasn't sure that this was such a great thing to be meeting up with him again. She decided to act a little smug, determined not to get too friendly.

Adam sensed her reservation and began to try to break the ice with conversation.

"How's your father?"

"Fine," she answered shortly.

"And your mother?"

"Fine too."

"And you Rose?"

"Fine."

Rose was looking for a way to escape this conversation. She wanted it to show that she was not pleased with him.

"Well, we are here already. This is where you may get ready for the show. I sure would like more time to visit with you, Rose. I'll catch up with you later. Good luck!"

"Thanks."

Rose found it most difficult to give him the cold shoulder. He was so polite and so very handsome! But she managed and closed the door abruptly to her dressing room.

ക്ക്ക്ക

The USO show had begun. Big name Hollywood stars were there to entertain. Hollywood studios, in between film commitments, sent their stars. This kind of show was the biggest production in the history of show business. Those involved in show business made a huge contribution to the war effort. This all contributed to a widespread national effort to help the troops.

The show was made up of musicians, comedians, and entertainers of all sorts on a make-do stage with thousands of GIs surrounding it. A singer began to beat out the saga of Boogie Woogie Bugle Boy of Company B.

USO night also included a grand variety of tap dancers, singers, pianists, song and dance vaudevillians, comedy teams, and big band music.

Near the end of the evening, they held the USO Queen competition. It was a very significant event. There were many beautiful girls. Rose felt honored to be involved. She wasn't expecting to win or to even place in the top five. She didn't feel a bit nervous inside. After all, she was just there to have a good time and to help entertain the GIs.

The GIs cheered and cheered as the Master of Ceremonies quickly narrowed it down to five candidates. It was pretty obvious who was their favorite by the way in which they applauded. Rose made it into the top five.

The crowd went wild as the top five finalists made their final walk on the deck. Rose couldn't believe that she had made it this far!

Adam was standing off to the right of the stage clapping, whistling, and cheering for Rose. She glanced over to look at him, and she caught his eye. He moved his lips to say, "You can do it!" and then smiled. Rose struggled to keep from smiling back, determined to keep a distance between them.

Rose saw Betty in the crowd cheering her on. Her heart beat faster, and now she was feeling the pressure.

"And the USO Queen title goes to, Miss Rose Krueger!" announced the Master of Ceremonies.

Rose couldn't believe what she was hearing. She let out a scream, and her hand came up to cover her mouth. She turned toward the other four girls, and they all embraced her in a circle with hugs.

Rose declared that this was the most exciting thing that has ever happened to her! This was even bigger that winning the Benton County Sweet Corn Queen contest back home! She glanced over to look at Adam, still uncertain as to whether it was such a good thing to have met up with him again.

Adam quickly came to her side. His job as her escort had become very important now for her own safety throughout the weekend on the base.

"Congratulations Rose!" Adam said as he embraced her for a brief moment. "You've done it again! What's it feel like to have won two queen contests in your lifetime?"

"I'm in shock! There are so many wonderful girls. I'm just lucky I guess!"

Rose backed away from him to distance herself. She couldn't believe that he was acting like nothing had ever happened.

"I have strict orders to stick close by you this weekend now that you have the USO title. It's for your own safety," he said. "That won't be a problem will it?"

"I—I gues—s not!"

"Good! I'll walk around with you so that the servicemen can meet you."

"I'd appreciated that. I wouldn't want to do that by myself."

Adam still didn't seem to suspect that Rose was angry about anything. He just kept on being very polite and courteous to her.

The crowd of servicemen also seemed polite and respectful to Rose as she mingled with Adam along side of her. Adam kept close by her, and he made sure that this was an enjoyable experience for Rose.

After the show was over and the evening was coming to an end, Adam said, "Rose, would you join me for a walk out on the pier?"

"I suppose so," answered Rose. "I need to unwind a little."

As they walked down by the pier together, Rose remained very quiet, secretly hoping that Adam would recognize that something was wrong and maybe ask her about it.

"Look at all of the servicemen leaning over the ship rails, waving, screaming, and cheering," Adam commented. "I wonder how many will be coming back."

Her thoughts turned to Wayne, wondering where he was and if he was safe. She remembered having to say goodbye to him. It wasn't easy. She understood the pain of all the men and their sweethearts having to say goodbye, not really knowing if they'd ever see one another again.

Sweethearts stood on the dock singing together as the ships sailed away to war. This was the worst war in the history of the world. Rose and Adam could here them singing the song, *Don't Sit Under The Apple Tree With Anyone Else But Me.*

"That's a song about a GI asking his girl to be true to him while he's gone," said Adam.

"Is that so," she spoke as her thoughts returned to Wayne. Would she be able to remain true to him or was she beginning to feel differently about Wayne and their relationship?

"Rose. A penny for your thoughts?"

She looked over at him, "Oh, I'm sorry, Adam. I was just thinking about a friend back home. Sometimes it's so hard to say goodbye."

"I know. That's why I left Iowa without saying goodbye to you. I don't say goodbye very well."

"Really? Is that why you left so quickly?"

"Yes, I'm sorry. Will you please forgive me?"

Rose looked at Adam as if a huge burden had been lifted off of her shoulders.

"Yes, I'll forgive you! I was really angry with you. I was trying to show it when I first met you again. Could you tell?"

"Yes."

"Will you forgive me for acting that way?"

"Certainly. I deserved it. Let's start over," he suggested. "I'm going up to Chestertown for the rest of the weekend where I went to college. They're having the annual Chestertown tea party festival. History comes to life during this celebration and I thought that you might like to come. It is a re-enactment of the event of 1774 when local colonists boarded the British ships and dumped their cargo of tea into the deep blue depths of the river. It's held on the banks of the Chester River," Adam explained with great enthusiasm. "Would you like to come?"

"Sure. That sounds like fun. This would be a great chance for me to get to see some more things in Maryland. I don't have any transportation to leave the school very often."

"I'd be happy to show you all around Maryland."

"Sounds good, Adam. I'm lucky to have met up with you again. I'm anxious to write back to my father and tell him."

"How has your father been after selling the farm?"

"He deeply regrets selling the farm, but he tries to be positive, realizing that if he hadn't done that, he wouldn't have had the money to help me come out here."

"Life has a funny way of working itself out, doesn't it, Rose?"
"You can say that again!"

CHAPTER 7: RED SAILS IN THE SUNSET

Chestertown was an area of rich history. Wealthy merchants built many of the town's grand homes back in the eighteenth and nineteenth centuries. Specialty shops, galleries, antique stores, and charming inns adorned the quaint cobblestone sidewalks along wide, shaded streets.

"Did I tell you that Weston College is one of the oldest liberal arts colleges in the country?" asked Adam. "Our country's first president helped establish it."

"That's impressive," replied Rose. "Oh, look at that beautiful little antique shop. Let's go in and look around."

"Maybe I can find something for you," said Adam. "A gift to congratulate you for winning the USO Queen contest."

"That's not necessary," she responded with a blush.

Adam found a great place to park the car for the day. There was so much to do and so much to see all in one area of town.

"We could leave the car here for the day and walk to just about everything," said Adam.

"That would be fine. I could use some exercise."

"Did you wear your comfortable shoes?"

"Nurses always wear comfortable shoes. I'm on my feet a lot."

They went inside the enchanting little shop, and they spent a great deal of time looking at all the beautiful things. It didn't take Rose long to decide that everything in the store was far too expensive for her limited budget as a student nurse.

Rose gasped, "Look at this exquisite silver cake server!"

"This was part of a collection made by the Safe Company. It was made by some of the original silversmiths in the history of our country right here in Maryland," said Adam. "I have purchased some for my mother."

"This is uniquely gorgeous stuff," said Rose. "Look at the sterling silver handle decorated with rosettes and flowers that climb up and down the entire handle."

"This is a unique piece," said Adam. "I'd like to buy it. It reminds me of you, Rose, with the handle so intricately shaped into a rose design. Look here on the flat part of the handle. This dates back to the beginning of our country. This is the perfect gift for you, Rose."

"You really know a lot about antiques, Adam," said Rose with amazement.

"I like history and I've spent some time reading about the history of our state. Tell the sales lady that we will take this and ask her to wrap it up."

"If you don't mind I'd like to ship this back to my mother in Iowa," said Rose.

"That's fine," said Adam. "I'll be right back."

Rose waited for the saleslady to get her gift ready. When she was finished, she turned to leave the shop and Adam, came up behind her with his hands behind his back.

"What are you hiding, Adam?" Rose questioned.

"It's a surprise," said Adam rather playfully.

"For what?"

"For later," he said. "Let's walk down the street to Woody's Crab House for lunch. They have the best crabs in the bay area."

They walked a little ways down the street, but Adam couldn't contain himself any longer. He was too excited about what he had found to give Rose. He pulled his hands out from behind his back and said, "Rose, this is for you!"

It was a small rectangular-shaped, white box. Rose carefully opened up the lid.

"Oh, Adam, it is beautiful," Rose answered.

Her eyes danced with excitement. It was a silver charm bracelet with a single rose charm dangling from it. The rose had a ruby stone in the center of it. It was the most wonderful gift that anyone had ever given her.

"I'll treasure it forever!" said Rose.

"This is for winning the USO Queen contest and it's my way of apologizing to you," he said.

"What are you apologizing for?" she asked.

"I felt very badly that I came into your life back in Iowa so quickly and bought out your family farmland for the bank that I worked for. I now realize how painful that must have been for you and your family. You come from a great family and I enjoyed getting to know them while I was there. Will you forgive me?"

"Yes, I'll forgive you. The good thing that came of it was that I was able to come to school out here. We had enough money to pay for what the Cadet Nurse Corps wouldn't cover."

"Yes, but I'm sure that your father still wonders if he did the right thing. I know how much you all wanted that farm to stay in the family."

"Yes, I still believe he is disappointed."

"Someday I will make it up to you and your family. I promise!"

Rose looked into his eyes and saw that he seemed very serious, but didn't see how that would ever be possible.

"I'll help you put on your bracelet so that you can wear it. When I saw it in that gift shop back there I couldn't believe it. It's perfect for you! You can add other charms that you collect while you are out here for school."

"Thank you. This is very special."

Rose suddenly realized that this man from the east was a soft, gentle, and sensitive man. He was extremely intelligent, and she found him to be very interesting. She began to soak in all that he was showing and telling her about this part of the country. It was like having your own personal history teacher. Adam treated her as if she were someone special. Rose liked that a lot.

Lunch at Woody's Crab House was a delightful experience. Adam convinced Rose to try the blue crab. He insisted that it tasted much better than other crab that is found in other parts of the country, such as stone crab and king crab.

Adam explained to Rose, "The preparation of the food is very interesting. They steam the crab in spices until it turns red. They will hand us mallets and we'll have fun cracking them open."

"It sounds kind of messy.'

"It can be," answered Adam, "but it's great fun! They creatively serve crab on everything here. They serve a delicious creamed vegetable crab soup, baseball-sized crab cakes with a special sauce, a Caesar salad with crab on top, and crab pasta."

"I suppose they even have crab desserts?" said Rose.

"They sure do," answered Adam. They serve crab-shaped chocolates for dessert."

Rose laughed in response to the detailed description of the crab house menu.

"I think I'll enjoy this food and the artful preparation of it," she said.

Adam and Rose really enjoyed their seafood lunch together. Adam was paying the bill at the cash register by the front door of the crab house, and he noticed a poster hanging up in the entryway.

"Rose! Come here and look at this."

"What is it Adam?"

"Weston is playing St. Mary's tonight at the university."

"You're kidding! I didn't know that they played one another in football."

"Let's go, Rose. That would be fun. I could show you where I played football and then we could go to my old hangout after the game!"

"Sounds like fun. Especially since they're playing my school," she added. "I won't know which one to yell for."

"I will," Adam firmly stated. "My team, of course!"

"Of course," Rose agreed. "Since I'm with you, I'll go along with that."

"We should probably decide where to stay tonight," Adam suggested. "There is a beautiful Inn here in Chestertown. They have really cozy rooms. We could get two that are side-by-side if you don't mind having to share a bathroom with other guests. That's how most Inns are set up."

"Share a bathroom with other people?" Rose questioned.

"Yes, all of the rooms are upstairs and then all the guests share one bathroom. Is that OK with you Rose?"

"Sure. I've just never stayed in one before."

"You'll love the way it's decorated, in lovely Victorian style."

"Sounds nice."

"Then in the morning we can meet for breakfast in the dining room right there."

"That would be great!"

While Adam finished up paying the tab at the crab house, he said, "Let's get the car and drive over to the Inn to register for the night."

"I'm not sure that I can afford to stay there," Rose said with uncertainty. "It sounds pretty fancy."

"Don't worry. I'll take care of it."

"Are you sure?"

"We have to stay somewhere tonight. I have a lot more to show you."

As they approached the historical Inn, Rose couldn't believe how beautiful it was. The entire exterior of the building was made out of red stone. It had a very large front porch on it with an elaborate lead-glass door that marked the entrance. They checked in and carried their bags upstairs to the rooms.

The inside of the Inn was spectacular. The decor was very elegant. Rose had never seen anything like it before. There was so much to look at. It was decorated in rich jewel-tones and a variety of textures. She just wanted to run her fingers across the fabrics of the furniture and the raised velvet wall coverings. Everything was so well-coordinated and the atmosphere was polished and refined.

"Rose, let's walk around outside the Inn for awhile. There are lots of nice gift shops to look through, right here."

"I think that I can manage to shop some more, but only to look this time. No more gifts, please."

"I promise. No more gifts except maybe just one more."

"What's that, Adam?"

"There's a candy shop just around the corner that I'd like to go into."

"A candy shop!"

"Yes, I like their fudge and I really like their black licorice buttons!"

"Black licorice?"

"It's the best black licorice around!"

"I'll give it a try."

They spent the entire afternoon going through the quaint shops in the surrounding area. Rose even found that she liked the black licorice buttons that Adam had bought in the candy shop. One button would seem to last forever, just like she was secretly wishing that her weekend with Adam would last.

❧❧❧

As evening approached, they made their way over to the college for the football game. Adam walked a swift pace, anxious to see the game. Rose had to walk quickly to keep up. He hadn't been back for a football game as an alumnus for a long time. He was hoping that he would run into someone that he knew.

They walked past the Theta Kappa Nu Fraternity house. "I was a member of that fraternity," Adam pointed out. "I had some great times there."

"I bet you did," Rose commented. "I've heard a lot about what goes on in a fraternity!"

"It was all harmless fun."

"That's one opportunity that I won't have as a nursing student."

"What's that?"

"Being able to join a sorority."

"Oh, that's right, but you'll have other opportunities that I didn't have."

"Probably so."

They walked into the football stadium. "Let's find a good seat before it fills up," he said. "Wow, this seems strange to come back for a game. It feels good to be back here in this old place."

"What position did you play, Adam?"

"Tackle."

"Oh, you were a tough guy?"

"I was about a one-hundred-eighty seven pound, six-foot-two. tough guy back then."

"What number were you?"

"Number seventy-two"

"That sounds like a lucky number," she said. "What other teams did you play besides St. Mary's?"

"Back then we played Delaware, Loyola, Dickinson, Easton, Western Maryland, and some others. I'm not sure who they all play now."

"Did they always play St. Mary's?"

"You know, I'm not sure. We did when I was playing. That's all I know."

The game began and Adam and Rose enjoyed the excitement of the two teams striving for a victory on that beautiful fall day. The leaves were stunning in the assortment of fall colors that they displayed.

"Hey, Scoop!" someone yelled from behind Adam.

Adam turned around to see who was calling for him by his old college nickname. A few rows behind him sat a group of his old college football buddies.

"Hey, what are you guys doing here?" Adam turned to Rose, "Come on. Let's go up and see these guys. I'd like to introduce you to them."

Adam grabbed her hand and helped her step up the bleachers to where they were sitting. There was quite a group of them.

"Guys, I'd like you to meet Rose."

"Hi Rose!" they all said in unison.

"Rose, meet the guys. Here is Smith, Kirky, and Collins. Hoppe and Watson."

"It's nice to meet all of you. I've heard about some of you already," Rose acknowledged.

"Looks like you've gotten better taste in women, Scoop," teased Kirky.

"Well, actually, Rose and I have just become friends very recently. It's kind of a complicated story."

"Say, Scoop, we're all going down to the Cottage Inn after the game to listen to the Chatterbox Band. Would you two like to join us?"

"Well, I don't know if Rose would like that place," Adam said as he looked at Rose.

"I'll try it," she said. "I'm sure you'd like to visit more with your friends."

"OK. We'll see you there."

Adam and Rose went back to their seats and finished watching the rest of the game.

"My friend Kirky back there was really a good football player."

"Was he your best friend that you were telling me about when I first met you back in Iowa?"

"Yes, that's him. He was an All-American guard."

"Do you guys keep in touch?"

"Yes, but I don't keep in touch much with the other guys that you met. We've all gone in different directions, I guess."

"That same thing has happened to me and my friends too. But I plan to do a better job keeping in touch with them in the future."

The game turned out to be very exciting. This was a game where you stood up and down constantly and yelled until your voice got hoarse. Weston ended up winning by 3 points after kicking a very long field goal in the last minute of the game.

Adam and Rose went down to the Cottage Inn to meet up with the rest of the guys. Rose ended up feeling a little uncomfortable there. It was kind of a sports hangout where lots of men were re-hashing every play of the game. Adam could sense that Rose was getting very bored, so they decided to call it a night and say good-bye to the guys.

They each settled down in their own rooms for the night back at the Inn. Rose was very tired, and her feet hurt from all of the walking that they had done all over Chestertown. Her room was a very cozy place. The bed felt like a feather bed and her pillow was just as soft. A beautiful hand made quilt was draped over the bed. Rose felt like she was being treated like a queen, and as soon as her head hit the pillow, she fell asleep.

Rose woke up by a knock on the door. "It's time for breakfast. I'll meet you downstairs in fifteen minutes," Adam announced.

"I'll be there," Rose answered as she struggled to get out of the comfortable bed. It was a lot more comfortable than her dorm-room bunk-bed.

Rose walked down the big staircase that was lined in burgundy velvet wallpaper that lead to the dining area. Adam was waiting there for her, reading the morning newspaper and enjoying a cup of coffee.

"Good morning, Rose," Adam cheerfully greeted. "Did you sleep well?"

"I did. I wish my bed in the dorm was as comfortable!"

"Have a seat," he said as he put down the newspaper. "I have an idea for something that we could do today," offered Adam.

"What might that be?"

"We could go sailing on a chartered boat."

"I've never been sailing. I don't swim very well."

"Don't worry. I can swim. I used to be a Red Cross swimming instructor in college. I taught lessons during the summer to make extra money for school. There are life-jackets on the charter and the crew is well- trained."

"Fair enough. I guess I'll have to trust you once again."

Kent Island is where they ended up going to catch a charter shortly after lunch. They spent the afternoon sailing along the Eastern Shore. The waters were fairly smooth, and it was very relaxing. Rose decided that she loved to be on the water as long as she was in a boat and not swimming in it.

"There's a certain feeling you get when you're out on the *wooder*, isn't there Rose?"

"Yes, a feeling of serenity."

"I love the feeling," said Adam.

"I can understand it now. Being from the Mid-West, I've never known the tranquility that comes from being out on a sailboat on the Eastern Shore. You are lucky to have grown up here."

"Don't ever take for granted where you grew up, Rose. You may not have grown up by the *wooder*, but you had different kinds of things to give you the same feeling of peace and serenity."

"Like what?"

"I remember very well how it felt to sit on your front porch swing at the farm at dusk and listen to all of the sounds of the country. That was peaceful. That was a calm night that I really enjoyed."

"You're right, but I love your world too."

"And I like yours."

They watched the sun go down. The sunset was an outstanding display of yellow, orange, and reddish-orange hues.

"It's getting late. I'd better get you back to the school," said Adam.

"Yes, I suppose so, but it's so beautiful here. I'm not ready to go back. I've had such a beautiful day. Thanks Adam. You're really fun to be with."

They traveled back to Baltimore late into the evening, back to the dormitory and back to the routine of life.

As they were driving, Adam looked to Rose and said, "Did you leave anyone back home?"

"What do you mean, Adam?"

"I mean did you leave anyone special back home?"

Rose paused, "Yes, I did. I have a special friend back home. Why do you ask?"

"I just had this feeling that you did."

"He's not actually back home right now. He's been drafted into the Army. He wanted to stay at home and farm with his father until he got his call. I'm not sure what is going to happen now. Everything is so uncertain."

"What is his name, Rose?"

"Wayne Johnson."

"How do you feel about him?"

"I'm not sure anymore. He's a very nice person, and he thinks a lot of me. It's just that our lives seem to be going off in different directions. I'm confused about our relationship and our future. How about you, is there someone special in your life right now?"

"Oh, I date a few girls now and then," he said.

"Any of them significant?" Rose pressed.

"Maybe one is, or was, I mean. We've dated off and on since college."

Rose felt disappointed. She knew that she had Wayne back home, but she didn't expect to hear that Adam had someone in the background. But then why shouldn't he? He was a very handsome man with a lot going for him. They both became very quiet for the rest of the drive.

Adam pulled up in front of the school and walked Rose up to her dorm room. He turned to look at her face-to-face and said, "I really enjoyed your company this weekend."

"I enjoyed yours. Thanks for everything, Adam."

He picked up her hands and held them in his. Looking her in the eyes he said, " I really would enjoy showing you around again." He drew her near to him, and he gave her a hug. "Good night, Rose," he said as he softly kissed her cheek.

"Good night Adam," she said wondering if she really would ever see him again.

Rose turned to open the door to her room. She turned back for one more glance at him, but he was gone.

CHAPTER 8: KISS ME AGAIN

The events of the following week were pretty much as usual—class, study time, meals, and floor duty. Rose had already decided that she liked the surgical area of the hospital the best. She thought that she would like to become a head nurse in that department.

After a long day of school, Rose put up her feet to relax in the student lounge. She decided to open her mail from home. There was a letter from her mother. She really enjoyed getting letters from her. She was good at keeping her up on news about her high school classmates and what they were doing. Her mother and her friends' mothers all got together for coffee regularly, back home.

On this particular day, her mother's letter sounded different...

Dear Rose,

I don't want to alarm you, but I have not been feeling well lately. I've been so tired. I can barely get myself going in the morning. My energy level slowly increases as the day goes by. I went to the doctor last week and they said that I was anemic again. I've been anemic for some time now and it remains a mystery to the doctor. After giving it a lot of thought, I've decided to get a second opinion next week. I grow more and more concerned as time passes. Try not to worry about me. I will let you know more next week. I hope that your schooling is going well. I miss you!

Love,
Mother

Rose, determined more than ever to go see her mother, decided to take the train home, but it wasn't leaving until the following week. She was making plans to go back home when the telephone rang.

"Rose, it's me, Adam. Would you like to join me for a trip to Ocean City for the weekend? Maybe your roommate Betty would like to come along. I'll take my friend Kirky. Remember him from the football game at Weston College?"

"Well, I don't know. I just got a letter from my mother that really has me worried."

"Coming along with us for the weekend just might take your mind off of it for now. What do you say, Rose? Will you come?"

"I guess that I could. I can't get on the train until next week anyway. I'll talk to Betty. When will you be coming?"

"I'll pick you two up out in front of the dormitory at 8:00 in the morning," said Adam. "Be prepared to do some more boating. You're experienced at it now."

The trip to Ocean City sounded like a good idea to Rose. She'd been worrying so much about her mother. She felt like she couldn't get home soon enough. She welcomed this invitation and hoped that it would serve as a distraction to her worries.

കൗകൗകൗ

The trip to the ocean was a beautiful one. Rose longed to see more of the East Coast. It was every bit as nostalgic as she had thought it would be. Betty wasn't so impressed. She had grown up in the area, so this was nothing new to her.

"Just where is Ocean City? Asked Rose.

"Where the Atlantic surf meets the shore is this wonderful little resort town called Ocean City," explained Adam. "First there is the city, then the ocean boardwalk, which is three miles long. Then come the beach and the bay."

"The beach must go on for miles," said Rose. "I'd like to just lay on the beach and sunbathe first."

"So would I," agreed Betty.

"I guess it's two against one. Let's see what Kirky wants to do," said Adam as he turned to get his opinion.

"That's fine with me. I wouldn't mind working on a tan."

The beach was sensational that day. They made occasional dips in the surf, and they delighted in the saltwater splashing up against their bodies. They listened to the cry of the seagulls, and they enjoyed making sandcastles in the sand.

Adam and Kirky went up to the boardwalk and rented rafts. They had fun riding the waves with the rafts and pounding into the shoreline. Rose stayed close to the shoreline since she didn't swim that well.

"Let's go up on the boardwalk and have a soda," suggested Adam.

"That sounds good! I think I'll order the biggest one they make," said Rose.

The suggestion sounded good to Kirky and Betty as well. After a long time in the sun, they were all very thirsty.

The boardwalk was so full of things to see. They elected to spend the evening bicycling up and down the boardwalk viewing the interesting shops, the hotels, and the restaurants. They stopped at the Purple Moose Saloon for some live entertainment.

Later they dined at Fisherman's Wharf overlooking the inlet and indulged in a meal of fresh seafood topped off with pecan pie.

"I'm ready to call it a day," remarked Rose. "Where did you make arrangements for us to stay?"

"I've made reservation at the Surf and Sands Ocean Front Motel," answered Adam. "I've reserved two rooms, one for you girls and one for Kirky and I. The beach front of the motel has a unique feature to it that I think you'll enjoy. We can all sit around a fire on the beach and roast marshmallows and have hot chocolate."

"Adam, you're such an imaginative guy. Where have you been hiding this quality?"

"I recently just found a reason to be imaginative, I guess." Adam smirked as he looked at Rose out of the corner of his eye. "I wanted the perfect ending to a perfect day at the beach."

ॐॐॐ

The next day brought a new and exciting adventure. Rose was beginning to realize that she loved adventure like this, and it had definitely succeeded in distracting her from worrying about her mother and the need to go back home.

Ocean City was the white marlin capitol of the world. They all agreed to go deep-sea fishing for marlins.

A big forty-two-foot boat called *The Huntress* was available that day with a captain and his mate. They left the pier with great expectations. There was just one thing that they didn't count on.

"I feel sea sick!" exclaimed Rose.

"Here's a bucket," Betty said as she handed it over to Rose.

"This didn't happen to me before, Adam, when we went on the sail boat."

"Those were calmer *wooders*. This is the ocean in full strength today. Just have a seat for awhile, Rose."

Rose spent most of the day hanging her head over a fishy smelling bucket with her stomach in turmoil. The rest of the gang enjoyed the bright blue water splashing up against the side of the boat.

After several hours of being strapped to a chair in the back of the boat, hanging on to a huge fishing rod, Adam shouted, "I think I've got a big one!"

Adam called for Kirky to help grab a hold of the rod. Together they reeled in the big fish. It was a spectacular sight! They had caught a monstrous marlin!

"Wow, Adam!" Kirky roared. "You really did it this time. This has to be one of the biggest fish ever caught here in these waters. Look at the size of that thing!"

"I'm impressed," added Rose. "We don't catch fish that big back in Iowa."

"I'm usually not this lucky," said Adam. "There must be a secret good luck charm on board." Adam turned to glance at Rose.

"This has been a grand weekend!" said Rose. "Congratulations on the catch of the day!"

৵৵৵

They returned to the dorm late that evening, exhausted from the weekend. They all had so much fun together. Rose thought that Betty was beginning to find Kirky rather charming. She thought that it would be nice to do something together again sometime. This would present a less threatening atmosphere since she still had Wayne back home.

Rose began to think about her relationship with Wayne and her new friendship with Adam at school. Her direction in life seemed to be taking another turn. She became more puzzled as she spent more time with Adam.

৵৵৵

It was the middle of the week, and the long awaited letter from home had arrived. Her mother had gotten her test results back. Grace was amazed at how quickly they found out why she was not feeling well. Rose had wanted her to get a second opinion a long time ago, but her mother was content with her regular doctor.

Her mother did not reveal any specifics in her letter, but she indicated that a trip home would be a good idea if Rose could get excused from school.

Rose felt a familiar chill go up and down her body. She decided to pack her bags. In just a short time, Rose arrived at the train station trying to get on the next train home.

While she waited at the train station, she gave Adam a call.
"I'll be right over," said Adam
"Oh Adam, that's not necessary. I'll be all right."
"I insist! I want to come over to see you off."

"OK, I'll be here for another hour or so. I'll see you soon."

It wasn't more than twenty minutes later when his tall and slim figure came through the doorway.

"Hello, Adam," said Rose warmly in appreciation for his concern. "It was very nice of you to come. I'm very worried about my mother. She wouldn't say what the doctors found out in her letter."

"I understand. Say hello to her from me when you get home."

"I will," replied Rose. Her eyes became moist.

"Call me when you get back and I'll come and get you at the station."

"OK."

Adam sat with Rose on a bench. Not many words were spoken, but Rose knew by his presence that he cared, and she was thankful for that.

"All aboard," announced the conductor.

Adam reached over and gave Rose a kiss and said, "I've really enjoyed our time together. I hope that your mother is going to be OK."

"Thanks for everything," said Rose. She turned to embrace him.

Rose boarded the train and found a window seat. She waved to Adam, and the train rolled off into the western sunset. Adam stood there and watched until the train became lost in the pastel colors of the horizon.

✄✄✄

Conrad was waiting at the train station when she arrived. The train pulled up, and Rose ran out, excited to see her father. Her father placed his arm around her as they walked to the car together.

They drove back to the farm. Her father told her something that she would never forget.

"Rose, your mother is terminal."

"What do you mean terminal?" asked Rose in a trembling voice.

98

Her father answered while trying to hold back the tears, "It means that there is no cure for her illness."

"No cure?" Rose found it difficult to speak. Her voice was unsteady and bending.

"It's too advanced at this point," said her father.

"How much time does she have," asked Rose.

"The doctor said that she might only have a few months."

Rose sat back in her seat. She had so many questions, but she couldn't find the strength to ask them. The stillness of the night grew heavy.

After what seemed like a long trip home, they walked into the farmhouse. Rose ran to her mother's side. Tears streamed down her face as they embraced one another.

"Mother, I'm so sorry," Rose whispered. She stood back and looked at her mother.

"It's OK, Rose," said her mother with confidence in her voice. "I'm going to beat this. I'll fight it with all I've got!"

Her words helped Rose refrain the tears. They both began to talk. They talked late into the evening about Baltimore and all of the things that she had seen. Rose told her mother about Adam and all about the friendship that they had developed.

"Rose, don't forget about Wayne," her mother reminded. "I run into his mother often and she tells me that he's still waiting for you to come back home and marry him someday."

"I know. I've become even more confused about Wayne and how I feel about him. I have feelings for Adam now, Mother. He's so different from Wayne. I'm not sure that I want to come back and marry Wayne. I used to think that I might, but now that I'm away from home, things are becoming very different. Wayne still writes to me and he still seems so sure of what he wants, but I'm still not sure. I guess I've never really been sure."

"Rose, your father and I were really hoping that you would eventually come back and marry Wayne. There, I just said what I've been wanting to say for along time."

"I know that is what you and Father want, but doesn't it matter what I want?"

"Well of course, but Adam is very different."

"That is what I like about him, Mother. Actually, he is a lot like me!"

"But he isn't a farmer and he isn't a Lutheran," said her mother.

"Mother, I can see that we still don't see eye to eye on this matter, but let's not argue anymore about this. Right now it's you that I am concerned about. You're going to need me in the days to come and I'll be 1000 miles away. Maybe I should quit school for this semester and stay home and help you."

"Your father and I have worked it all out. The ladies in the church have offered to help me if I need it. I have many friends to call on. Don't you worry about me," said her mother. "I'll be fine. You just concentrate on finishing your schooling."

"But Mother!"

"I'm going to beat this illness, you'll see," said her mother. "Your father will take good care of me."

"I'll still worry about you," replied Rose. "I'll call you as often as I can. At least I can help you while I'm home now for a while. I'll see to it that you get things worked out before I go back."

Rose found that her time at home passed far too quickly. She arranged for someone to come in to help with the cleaning and the cooking. Rose spent many hours visiting with her mother, treasuring every moment that they had together.

✦✦✦

The time had come for Rose to go back to Baltimore. She clung to the hope that her mother would beat her illness in spite of the terminal diagnosis. There were so many unknown details about the illness and the course that it would take. Rose found that no one was willing to share much about it. This increased her anxiety.

━✦━✦━✦━

Rose returned to school and began spending a lot of time in the college library. She researched her mother's illness. She also tried to find out information on what to expect in the months to follow. Her research resulted in many dead-ends. This created a lot of frustration for Rose. She even asked the opinions of several of her instructors. Everyone that she asked was reluctant to make any predictions about what course her mother's illness might take. They all seemed to say the same thing, that it was different for every individual. But Rose continued searching for answers.

Eventually, Rose began to look for experimental treatments that were being done around the country. She would then immediately telegram her mother and tell her about her findings. Her mother's answer was always the same.

"I like my own doctor and I'm perfectly happy with my treatment here. I'm still hoping for a miracle," she would say.

Rose was looking at this whole situation from a different perspective than her mother. Rose accepted the possibility that her mother might die from this illness. Rose wanted to prepare herself for what might happen, but she also shared in her mother's hope for a miracle. Her mother loved life, and she would not accept a terminal diagnosis. She was a survivor, and it was reflected in her positive attitude.

On many occasions, Rose would send a gift back to her mother to keep her spirits lifted. Other times, she would just send a card with a note of encouragement.

Money was becoming scarce for Rose because of all of the calls she was making and the gifts she was sending back home. Rose was aware of the sizable debt that was mounting, but she rationalized it by saying that her mother might not be around much longer. She considered a part-time job to help keep up with the extra expenses.

Suddenly, Rose remembered that she hadn't called Adam since she had gotten back. She reasoned that it was about time to take a break from the all-consuming thoughts about her mother and her illness. She picked up the telephone and began to dial.

"Hello Adam, this is Rose. I'm back," she said rather sheepishly. "I've actually been back for a while, but I've been so busy catching up with school work and all, that I haven't had a chance to call you."

"Rose, I'm so glad to hear from you!" Adam enthusiastically replied. I thought that I might be gone by the time you called. I'm waiting for deployment to the arctic region. Are you free tonight?"

"Yes and I'd love to see you. What do you want to do?"

"I'd like you to meet my parents for supper. What do you think about that?"

"I'd be happy to meet your parents," answered Rose. "I've got so much to talk to you about."

"We can talk on the way over to their house," suggested Adam. 'I'll be over to pick you up around five."

∾∾∾

Adam picked up Rose in his blue Oldsmobile. Rose bolted out to his car and jumped inside.

"Adam—I missed you!"

" I missed you too!"

"Adam, there is something that I really need to tell you right now!"

"OK. Let's get down the road a bit and you can talk and I'll listen."

Rose couldn't contain herself for very long.

"Adam, my mother is very sick."

"How sick?"

"It's doesn't look good," said Rose with a trembling voice. "She's terminal! She doesn't have much time and here I am a thousand miles away and completely helpless!"

"Rose, you're not completely helpless. You can write to her and call her," he suggested.

" That's not the same as being right there with her. I want to quit school for the semester and go back home to be with her, but she insists that I stay and finish. What should I do?"

"Wow, that's a tough decision. Let's give it some more thought. We can talk about it again after we are finished meeting my parents. We're here. Let's go in and meet them. Are you going to be all right?"

"I'll be fine," she said as she tried to wipe away any signs of tears in her eyes.

They pulled up to a block of row houses on a street called Oakford Avenue. Rose was so busy talking to Adam about her mother that she forgot about the jitters that she had been experiencing before meeting his parents.

"My mother is a little outspoken," warned Adam. "My father is very easy to get to know though."

"I understand," said Rose. "My father is outspoken too. I'm used to it."

They walked up on the front porch and went in the front door.

"Hello, Mother," Adam said as he reached to give his mother a hug. "Mother, I would like you to meet Rose."

"Hello, Rose," she said as she held out her hand for a firm shake.

"It's very nice to meet you, Mrs. Waterman," replied Rose.

"Father, this is my favorite USO Queen," Adam introduced Rose with great admiration and respect.

"It's a pleasure to meet you, Rose. I've heard a great deal about you," said his father.

"Don't let her fool you Adam," interrupted his mother. "She's pretty and thin now but wait until she gets older. Look at her big bones!"

"Mother, how could you say such a thing?" Adam rolled his eyes at Rose and said, "Rose, never mind my mother. She really is a nice person."

Rose looked a little pale, but she took the remark very well.

"Let's all have a seat at the table and see if my mother can make up for that comment with a good meal," said Adam gently directing everyone over to the table.

Rose sat down next to Adam and his father, being cautious of his mother. His mother was a stern and rather large-framed woman with a glint of spitfire in her eyes. She continued to dominate the dinner conversation but Adam's kind and gentle father made up for it.

Adam's father was a retired carpenter. He stood shorter than his wife, and he seemed to let his wife take the lead. Adam showed equal respect for both of his parents, but he seemed to be more like his father.

Mrs. Waterman was a good cook. It was very apparent in the meal that she made. It was a delicious home-cooked Maryland style meal, and Rose really enjoyed it.

The table was set with the beautiful silver that Adam had found in the antique store in Chestertown. It looked spectacular and this reminded Rose to tell Adam how much her mother enjoyed the matching cake server that he had purchased for her. Adam's mother perked up to listen as they talked about the matching cake server.

"You gave a matching cake server to Rose that was part of my set?" his mother blurted out.

"Oh mother, it was just one piece out of the collection that I found and decided to let Rose send it home to her mother. You'll live without it. You never knew that it existed before now and you were fine. Her mother hasn't been feeling well and she wanted to send her a gift to cheer her up."

Rose was surprised at the way in which Adam stood up to his mother and was able to calm her down when needed. All in all, meeting Adam's parents was a success. Rose left his parent's home that evening with a certain feeling of satisfaction. She was beginning to understand this man that she found so intriguing when she first laid eyes on him back in the gazebo in Benton County, Iowa. She remembered how they spent the evening dancing to the music at the Sweet Corn Festival and how she felt attracted to him that very first night. Now here they were in Baltimore, Maryland, and he was taking her home to meet his parents.

They talked all the way back to the school that evening about their families. Rose shared a lot about her concern for her mother and her illness.

"Rose, there is something that I want to tell you. I lost my younger sister a few years ago. It had a great effect on my mother. My mother has seemed like a very angry and unhappy person since she died. I'm sorry if she hurt your feelings tonight. She seems to take out her frustrations on other people at times. I'm sorry that it had to be you," Adam spoke with great sincerity. "I think that she really liked you Rose, but it would be hard for you to tell since you just met her. Give her some time and hopefully, she will soften."

"Adam, would you share with me your experiences when your sister died? Maybe it would help calm my fear about the whole thing. I can't seem to find any straight-forward answers. There is no one willing to talk to me about it," said Rose.

"Sure, any time that you want to talk about it I'm here for you."

"Adam, I'm forever grateful. Just knowing that I have someone to talk to gives me peace. I'm still hoping for a miracle. But this way I can be prepared for whatever course it takes."

Rose looked at this man who had come into her life in such a strange way, as a real blessing. First, he helped her get to the college of her dreams, and now they had formed a deep friendship that gave her strength to make it through the challenging road that lie ahead.

"Rose, I would like to pick you up for church tomorrow. I think that you owe me this since the last time that we were in the same church together you hit me in the arm with a rolling pin!" teased Adam.

"How could I ever forget?" Rose remarked. "That was one of the most embarrassing moments of my life!"

Once again Adam walked Rose up to her dorm room. This path was becoming a familiar one.

"Goodnight Rose," he said as he reached over to give her a kiss.

"Adam, kiss me again!"

CHAPTER 9: LET ME CALL YOU SWEETHEART

"Your church is very different from my church back home," Rose remarked.

"In what way?" asked Adam.

"Back home we recite a lot of liturgy and sing strong hymns that have the feel of a march. Your hymns are more upbeat in tempo and I'm amazed at how the people feel free enough to clap their hands while they sing. I wouldn't dream of clapping my hands to our hymns."

"Why not?"

"It just wouldn't be appropriate!" she said.

"Did you feel uncomfortable, Rose?"

"Maybe a little," she admitted. "But even though the style of church is not one that I'm familiar with, I kind of liked it. But my parents would never approve. They have made it very clear that they'd like me to stay in the Lutheran church."

Adam answered politely, "I'm not trying to convert you. I just wanted you to come and see where I go to church."

"I know. But I really liked it! I'd go again."

"I've brought along a picnic lunch," said Adam. "I know a great place to have a picnic. I'll surprise you!"

"Sounds swell! You can sure come up with some neat things to do," said Rose.

As they drove away from the church they began to really enjoy discussing the sermon. Rose liked to do this with her father after church on Sunday mornings. He loved to quiz her to see if she was really listening. She felt right at home when Adam started to do the same thing. Adam came from such a different background, yet he seemed so familiar.

Adam approached a state park on the Chesapeake, and they came upon a picturesque spot where they stopped to have lunch.

"Look at that charming little gazebo over there," said Rose. "We should have our lunch in it. It looks like the gazebo back home in the park where we first met."

"It looks like this one is made out of red cedar," Adam commented. " It sure has a lot of detail. It's very beautiful."

Adam lifted the picnic basket out of the car and they walked over to the gazebo.

"It has a memorial plaque hung up on the railing," Adam noticed. "It says: in Memory of My Beloved."

"Someone must have built this gazebo as a memorial for this park," said Rose. "What a nice idea!"

"Gazebos are neat," said Adam. "They really make a park look quaint. I'm getting hungry. How about you?"

"Yes, what are we having?"

"I have crab-salad sandwiches, carrots, and crab dip, crabapples and crab-shaped cookies for dessert," Adam said as he carefully unpacked the food and spread it out on the picnic table.

"I guess I know what your favorite food is," Rose chuckled. "I'm not sure that I want to eat any crabapples, though!"

"I was just kidding about the crabapples," said Adam. "I don't even know if you can really eat them."

"I don't know either, but I do know that eating lunch in a gazebo overlooking the Chesapeake is a great way to spend a Sunday afternoon."

"Let's walk over to the *wooder*. There is something that I want to show you," said Adam.

"Is it that beautiful lighthouse over there?"

"Yes it is. Lighthouses have a fascinating role in maritime architectural history," Adam explained. "The first lighthouse in Maryland was built in 1822. There must be thirty or forty lighthouses on the bay, each with their own unique architecture."

"What's this particular one called?" asked Rose

"This one is called a screw-pile style lighthouse. It resembles a cottage on stilts. The base screws into the sandy depths of the bay."

"Can we go in?"

"I think so," said Adam. "The view from the inside is incredible. It stretches out for miles and miles out over the *wooder*."

The sky was a beautiful shade of blue. The view was captivating and thought-provoking as they stood there overlooking the water from high up in the lighthouse, breathing in the smell of the fresh air rolling into the bay.

"Rose, I'll be leaving on deployment soon," said Adam as he turned to look in her eyes.

"How soon?"

"I don't know. It will come without warning."

"You might have to leave without saying goodbye again?"

"That's right," he confirmed.

"But that's not fair!" she protested.

"I know. It doesn't seem fair at all!" Adam took Rose by the hand. "I have grown to like you a great deal in the past few months and I don't want to leave now. It seems like we're just beginning to get to know each other. I've never met anyone like you."

Rose didn't know exactly how to respond to him. She wanted so much to hear this, but there was Wayne.

"I've grown to like you a lot too," Rose agreed.

"I'll miss you, Rose."

"I'll miss you too, Adam. You're like this lighthouse—a beacon shining in my life."

Adam pulled her closer to him and said, "Rose…"

"What is it, Adam?"

"I'm falling in love with you!"

She looked into his eye, unable to resist his affection and answered, "I think I'm falling in love with you too!"

"What are we going to do, Rose?"

"About what?"

"About Wayne?"

"I don't know!" said Rose. "And my parents. They also want me to go back to Apple Grove and marry Wayne."

"You'll have to make a decision soon," he said.

"I know. I will—I promise!"

"Let me know when you've made it."

"You'll be the first to know."

"Most people are not as lucky as you, Rose."

"What do you mean?"

"You have two men that love you. Some people don't find one love in a lifetime!"

"What are you going to do about the girl that you've been seeing, Adam?"

"I've taken care of that already. It's over!"

࿇ ࿇ ࿇

Once again, Adam took Rose back to her dormitory. Feeling closer than ever before, they found it even more difficult to say goodbye this time. They had shared their true feelings for one another, and the situation became more complex. They parted that afternoon with uncertainty about their future.

Rose spent the evening studying in the student lounge, but her thoughts were very far away from the pages in the book that she was trying to read. She found that it was very difficult to concentrate.

࿇ ࿇ ࿇

Monday unfolded as usual. School assignments, projects and papers were beginning to pile up. Rose realized that she had to buckle down. The pressure was building. Rose spent most of her time trying to catch up on her homework assignments. She tried really hard to focus on school while trying to fight the temptation to constantly think about Adam.

❦ ❦ ❦

After several days of playing catch up on her schoolwork, Rose took a long overdue break to visit with Betty. Going out for lunch in the hospital cafeteria was one of their best ways to get some time to talk. Once again, Betty was there for her.

"How are things going, Rose? Are you getting caught up?"

"Yes, but I'm finding it hard to concentrate."

"Why is that?" asked Betty

"Well, it's Adam."

"What's wrong with Adam?"

"Nothing is wrong with Adam, it's just that, well, Betty…"

"What is it, Rose?"

"I've fallen in love with him!"

"Rose—you haven't?"

"Yes, I have. He's wonderful!"

"What about Wayne?"

"That's the problem, Betty. How am I going to tell him?"

"I don't know but you'd better tell him soon! You're going to break his heart."

"I know. That's why I have waited for so long. I've always feared that someday I would break his heart. I wanted to make sure that I really loved Adam and that he really loved me before I broke it off forever."

"How do you know that you really love Adam?"

"I just know. I can feel it. It's really hard to explain, but it's the kind of feeling I get when I'm around him. He also challenges me to grow."

"Rose, you're so lucky."

"Why?"

"Because I haven't even found one man that loves me and you have two!"

Rose laughed, "That's what Adam said. I'm going to call him tonight and tell him."

"Tell him what?"

"That I've decided to tell Wayne. I'm also going to tell my parents how I feel about Adam."

"Oh, Rose what do you think they will say?" asked Betty.

"I don't know, but they will soon know that I'm not coming back to marry Wayne Johnson! Not now and not ever! And I just might not stay in the Lutheran church either!"

"Rose, you'd better not tell them both of those things at the same time!" suggested Betty.

"Maybe you're right, Betty. I think that I'll wait on the church thing."

"That sounds like a good idea. Good luck, Rose!"

"Thanks. I'm going to need it!"

"Say, when was the last time you heard from Adam?"

"Ah, come to think of it, not for awhile!" she answered in a panic-stricken voice. "Something must be wrong! He hasn't called in a few days. Maybe I said something to give him the wrong impression of our relationship. Betty, I've got to go call him right now! See you later, and thanks for listening to me."

Quickly reaching for her purse, she excused herself and rushed out of the cafeteria and back to her room to call Adam. There was no answer. Rose kept trying to call until after so many unsuccessful attempts to reach him, she asked to borrow Betty's car to drive over to the base.

Rose left for Annapolis hoping to find him. She so desperately wanted to tell him that she had finally decided to break things off with Wayne once and for all.

Traffic thickened and Rose grew impatient. She was not used to driving in a lot of heavy traffic. She pulled herself closer and closer to the steering wheel and her hands tightly clutched the sides. Her knuckles began turning white as she fought back tears as long as she could. After a few deep breaths and a short prayer, Rose knew that she had to calm down and view the situation in a more rational manner.

Rose pulled up to the base and searched for the information center. An officer on duty attending the center gave Rose a map and directions to where Adam was staying.

Rose found the building on the base. She climbed up a long flight of steps to find his floor. Proceeding down the hall, Rose had to stop to catch her breath a few times until she found the door with the correct room number on it. On the right hand side of the door, she found a bulletin board attached to it. It had a note pinned to it that read:

The following officers have been deployed. We apologize to family members that we were unable to contact on such short notice. You may contact Officer Brown at headquarters office for information concerning the individual in question.

About halfway down the list was Adam's name. Rose felt her heart sink. There was so much that she wanted to say to him. She had kept so many of her feelings to herself. She finally knew how she truly felt, and now, he was gone!

Rose wondered if his parents even knew that he was gone yet. She decided to search for Officer Brown for more information.

Rose found the main office. It was the most impressive building on the base. Rose quickly scanned the directory in the main entryway to find Officer Brown. Still hopeful, she headed to his office, only to find a secretary that was reluctant to let her in to see him.

"Are you a family member, Miss Krueger?"

"No, but I'm a close friend of his."

"I'm sorry. We only give out information to family."

"But I must talk to Officer Brown," Rose insisted.

"I'm sorry," said the secretary.

"But I'm a very worried about him!"

"I have told you, Miss Krueger, only relatives may be given information about our officers," the secretary replied firmly. "I don't make the rules. I just abide by them."

"What's so secret about where he is?" asked Rose.

"He's been assigned to a top secret mission."

"Oh, I see."

Rose turned around, away from the secretaries desk, overcome with emotion, and slowly made her way back to the car.

The drive back to school felt like the longest ride that she had ever taken. The fear of never being able to see Adam again captured her thoughts. The beacon of light that had been shining in her life had quickly gone dim.

CHAPTER 10: MEMORIES

Rose arrived back at the dorm where Betty was anxiously waiting for her. She wanted to hear if Rose had found Adam. Betty could sense that something was terribly wrong the minute that she saw Rose.

"What happened, Rose?"

"Adam is gone!"

"Gone?" repeated Betty.

"He's already been deployed," said Rose

"Without any warning?"

"Yes, he told me that this might happen, but I guess I really didn't expect it to happen so soon. I've been so consumed with my mother's illness, that this caught me by surprise."

"I'm so sorry, Rose. I bet he'll get in touch with you somehow soon."

"I don't know, Betty. He's on a top-secret mission. This is just not good timing."

"What do you mean that it is not good timing?"

"I was just going to tell him that I have decided to break it off with Wayne."

"Try to be patient, Rose. He'll get a hold of you soon. I know he will."

Betty tried very hard to cheer her up. She had been successful at doing this in the past, but this situation was different. She couldn't seem to find just the right words to counsel Rose. Betty pulled up a chair and sat down in silence, sensing that there was nothing else to say.

৶৶৶

Many days had passed and there was no word from Adam. Rose received a telegram from her father. He wanted her to come back home soon. Her mother was experiencing some serious complications from her illness. He sent some money for the train ride home and a note for the school to excuse her for a family emergency.

This time it didn't take long for Rose to make the arrangements to get home. People seemed very helpful and understanding when they found out why she needed to get back.

On the thousand mile train ride, Rose thought a lot about how she might find her mother. She was preparing for the worst since she really didn't know what to expect. The train ride gave her a great deal of time to think about how she might be encouraging to her mother.

What will I say, she would ask herself over and over again? There were so many things that she wanted to talk to her mother about, but she couldn't find the words that would lead her into the conversation. The only thing that she felt comfortable saying to her mother was that she loved her. But would that be enough?

Rose wondered if she would be there for her mother in the last days of her life, since she was traveling back and forth to Baltimore. She wanted to be there, but she had to come to terms with the fact that she might not be.

Her father was waiting for her when she arrived at the train station. This time he didn't look so well. He looked tired and worn-down with a weary look on his face. Rose ran to greet him embracing him firmly.

"Father, I'm so happy to see you! It seemed like such a long way home," said Rose. "I thought that I would never get here!"

"I'm so glad that you have come home, Rose. Your mother has come down with pneumonia. It has complicated things. She is so weak and she has difficulty breathing. I've hired someone to come to the house to help me. I can't take care of her by myself anymore."

"I can help now that I'm home," Rose reassured her father. " I don't have to go back to school for a while."

Rose began to see just how weary her father had grown. She was so thankful that she came home to help. This is where she belonged.

They arrived at the farmhouse. Rose took a deep breath and then walked into the bedroom where her mother was. She found her mother very weak, but she managed to give Rose a smile. Her eyes lit up with excitement when she saw her daughter. Rose leaned over the bed to give her a hug and to finally feel her in her arms. It was a special moment that Rose would always remember.

"Rose, it's so nice of you to come home," her mother said in a soft voice struggling to speak. "I missed you so much! How is school and how is Adam?"

"School is fine mother, but I'm not sure how Adam is. He's been deployed on a special top-secret mission for the Navy. I didn't get a chance to say goodbye to him. He warned me that this could happen at any time, but I was still caught by surprise. I was shocked and disappointed when I tried to find him at the base."

"Have you heard from Wayne?" Asked her mother.

"Yes, I still continue to hear from him. He sends me very nice letters and still speaks of the day when we will both come back home to Apple Grove to get married. As I read those letters I feel more uncomfortable about that. Mother, there is something that I need to tell you."

"What is it, Rose?"

"I've decided that I don't want to marry Wayne after all," said Rose. "The more I get to know Adam, the more certain I am."

"Then you need to tell Wayne," replied her mother. "Tell him soon! You owe him the truth. You and Wayne have been dating for a long time. He loves you very much and it will take him time to get through the disappointment. We think so much of his family. Tell him soon, Rose."

"I will," she said. "I didn't plan on going off to school and finding Adam again. He just came into my life in the most unusual way. Our relationship began as a friendship and now it has become much more.

After meeting him at the county fair, I never dreamed that he would show up again in Maryland. He has always been there for me at just the right times."

"Rose, there are some things that I need to tell you too."

"Like what, Mother?"

"I'm very happy for you. I know that I've pushed for you to marry Wayne, and I confess that it was for all of the wrong reasons. I wanted you to marry a Lutheran boy from home. That was selfish of me. Please forgive me."

"I can't believe it, Mother! Do you mean you that I have your approval?"

"Yes, I've had time to give it a lot of thought lately. You are the only one who can decide whom you love. I want you to be happy. I also want you to be free to choose your own church and I'm sorry for being so demanding that you accept the traditions of the Lutheran church. The most important thing is that you are a believer, regardless of what denomination you attend."

"Are you sure, Mother?"

"Yes, I am sure. I love you, Rose."

"I love you too, Mother, and I am grateful for my Lutheran heritage. It has taught me about faith, which is what I am standing on to get me through these uncertain times," she said as she put her head down on her mother's shoulder. She wasn't ready to give her mother up yet. She wasn't sure that she ever would be. Her eyes became moist, realizing that her mother was losing this battle. Rose didn't want her mother to see her cry. She fought back the tears. She wanted to be strong for her. Soon, she would have to say goodbye.

Rose was able to get excused from school for a few more weeks. She spent a lot of time trying to run errands for her mother. Her mother would send her to town to get things for her. Grace still wanted to look pretty even though her skin was growing pale.

"Rose," her mother asked, "do you think that you could go into town and get me a pretty shade of lipstick?"

"Why sure, Mother, that would give me something to do for you. Is there anything else that I can get you?"

"I could use some lotion. My skin gets so dry."

"OK, I'll get that too. Anything else?"

"Maybe some new slacks. My pants are getting too tight."

"This will keep me busy for quite some time, Mother. Are you sure you'll be all right?"

"I'll be fine."

Rose knew that her mother liked to be left alone to sleep. She didn't mind running errands for her. In fact, it gave her a break to get out in the fresh air awhile. She didn't know if her mother was just trying to think of things for her to do or if she really needed these things.

Rose enjoyed going into town. There were a lot of friendly people that would ask her how her mother was doing. Rose would run into people that she hadn't seen for a while. Everyone asked her how school was going. She would just smile and say that things were fine.

After she had spent a good deal of time gathering all of her mother's requests, she went back out to the farm excited about finding her mother all sorts of things.

"Mother, look, I found you more that one pair of slacks in your size!"

"More than one pair?" her mother asked.

"Yes, I found a red pair, a purple pair, a black pair and a tan pair!"

"Wow, I'll be set for a long time."

"Is there anything else that I can get for you today?"

"No, but I would like you to come and sit here by my bed. Let's just visit a little while."

Her mother liked her to sit by her bedside and to help pass the long hours away. Rose would put on soft music to help comfort her. Grace would doze off a lot, and Rose spent a lot of time waiting for her to wake up. Rose took turns with her father sitting by her bedside. Once in awhile, one of her friends would come and give them both a break.

Grace lost strength and became bed-ridden very quickly. She was only able to raise her hands once in a while. Rose helped her to eat as her appetite grew slim.

"Can I get you some soup?" Rose asked her mother.

"Yes, soup sounds so good to me. What kind are we having tonight, Rose?"

"Creamy potato."

"That would be nice. Just a couple of bites will do. I get full so quickly."

"But, Mother, you have to eat to keep up your strength!"

"I will. I still get hungry."

Rose lifted the soup-spoon up to her mother's mouth and helped her take a bite. After just three spoonfuls her mother said, "Thanks, I've had enough."

"But Mother, you've only had three bites!"

"I'm full. It was really good."

Rose knew that her mother was desperately trying to eat to keep up her strength for as long as she could, but it was getting difficult. She simply just wasn't hungry anymore, and it took all that she had to take a few bites. Rose set the food aside.

Grace seemed to be resting comfortably in a half-asleep state. As Rose sat there next to her mother's bed, very spontaneously, her mother began to recite a prayer that she taught her when she was a small child.

"Mother, I used to say that prayer every night before I went to sleep," said Rose amazed that her mother was praying this prayer.

"You did?" asked her mother.

"Yes, and I wrote a song for it. Would you like to hear it?"

Her mother seemed to perk up, and she said with delight, "Sure, I'd love to hear you sing!"

Rose began to sing the song to her mother at her bedside. She fought back the tears. By the last line of the song, she could no longer hold them back. Now, for the first time, Grace began to cry too. Teardrops rolled down from the corners of her eyes.

"Mother, I'll miss you," Rose said with a broken voice.

"I'll miss you too!"

The room was silent for a while. There were tears but there was also peace.

"Rose, I'm ready now."

"Ready for what?" Rose asked looking into her mother's eyes.

"I'm ready to go home."

Rose kept silent, but she was glad in her heart that her mother had finally come to terms with her illness.

"We'll be together in heaven someday!" said her mother.

"I know. I'll look forward to that day," replied Rose.

Rose put her head down on the bed beside her mother. This was the special moment that she had been waiting for. It was her chance to say goodbye to her mother while she was still conscious, even though in her heart she knew that saying goodbye meant only for a little while.

Rose left her mother's bedside. She went out to the mailbox by the road in front of the farmhouse and noticed that there was a package tied to it. It was addressed to Rose Krueger from the U.S. Navy postal service. Rose quickly snatched it off of the mailbox and she ran into the house to open it.

"Father, I've gotten a package! I wonder if it's from Adam," said Rose. "I haven't heard a thing from him since he was deployed on his secret mission."

"Hurry up and open it!" said Conrad acting just as excited as Rose.

Rose slowly unwrapped the package, as if she wanted to savor the moment. She pulled out a short note:

Dear Rose,

Hello! How is everything? I'm so sorry that I didn't write much sooner. I've been so busy. You really must be wondering where I am. It all happened so fast. Not being able to say goodbye to you was very difficult for me. Please understand that I'm on a top-secret mission, but I miss you very much! I'm all right so don't worry about me. Give my love to your mother and father. I have sent you something to keep the bracelet in that I gave you. I will write again soon since I can't say what I want to right now anyway.

> *Love & Kisses,*
> *Adam*

Rose carefully opened up the small package. Inside was a tiny music box. She opened the lid and it began to play the song, *Gazebo Waltz*. This made her smile again as she remembered dancing with Adam to this song in the gazebo the night that they first met. Her beacon of light had reappeared in her life, and it felt good.

It was time to write to Wayne. She needed to tell him about Adam and that their relationship was over. She had been putting it off all too long. Now that she had heard from Adam she was ready to face her true feelings.

Rose sat down at the kitchen table and began to write a letter to Wayne. It was the most difficult letter that she had ever written. She really did care for Wayne, and they had so many special memories in high school together, but it was time to break it off, forever. After a lot of thought, she wrote:

Dear Wayne,

There is no easy way to give you this news. Please find it in your heart to forgive me someday.

I have been thinking about our relationship a lot lately and our future together. Since I have come out east to school I have changed a great deal. I have grown up a lot and have discovered who I am and what I want for my life.

I would like to end our relationship. Wayne, I'm very sorry, but I'll always have a special place in my heart for you. We've had some great times together that I will never forget!

Fondly,
Rose

Rose read the letter over and over again to make sure that it said exactly what she wanted it to say. She sealed it up, slipped the letter into the mailbox by the road near the farmhouse, and went off to show her mother the music box that she had gotten from Adam. The beautiful waltz that it played just might cheer her up, thought Rose.

Rose entered her room and looked over to see her mother lying on the bed. Tears gently dropped, one by one, picking up the pace down her soft cheeks. Her mother had lost consciousness.

She sat down in the chair beside her bed. She clutched the music box that she had brought for her mother to listen to. The room was perfectly still.

Slowly, Rose wound up the music box and let it play. She picked it up and held it up to her mother's ear. There was no visible response, but she believed that her mother could still hear.

The music played on…

CHAPTER 11: I'LL SEE YOU AGAIN

Rose boarded the train that took her back to Baltimore. Her father promised that he would come see her as soon as he felt up to it. It was hard for Rose to go back and leave her father at home to grieve alone. Adam wasn't there waiting for her, and she had no idea when she would ever see him again. She felt empty inside and began to question her purpose in life.

Rose really had to work hard to catch up and to complete her semester at school. The busier she kept the better. This left her with little time to feel sorry for herself.

∾❧∾❧∾❧

The semester had ended and Rose took the opportunity to take a break from school for the next term. The government was establishing a new overseas unit to travel with the USO camp show program. Rose was asked to join this special unit as the reigning USO Queen.

She got very excited about this and hoped that this was the opportunity that she had been looking for.

Rose found out that there were a number of girls from her dormitory that were also interested in this same opportunity, so they all got together and made the trip to Annapolis to find out more about it.

When the girls had arrived at the Naval base, an officer greeted them.

"The government is establishing a USO camp show program called, Over The Seas Unit Number One," said the officer. "We believe that entertainment should follow the forces wherever they go. Five new units are being sent out immediately to Newfoundland and other locations in the Arctic. Some units are headed to Alaska and other ones to Panama. Some are also being dispatched to the South Pacific, Bermuda, Iceland, Great Britain, and Australia. Are you ready and willing to serve your country?"

"Yes, Sir!" answered the girls in unison.

"It all sounds so exciting," said Rose.

"Good," said the officer. "You'll be an important part of each show as USO Queen, Rose. I hope that you will enjoy that role."

"I think I will. It sounds like the opportunity I've been looking for," answered Rose. "I'm ready to serve!"

Rose hadn't felt this excited about something for a long time. This opportunity seemed to be both adventurous and rewarding to Rose. She was anxious to put the sad and painful days of the past behind her. She could see the light and hope for the future, ready to go on with a renewed sense of enthusiasm. Her mission in life would now be to entertain the servicemen, helping to lift their spirits. The war effort marched on.

After a short orientation to the new unit of service that Rose would be involved in, the girls returned to the school with anxious feelings about their new commitment. They shared their fears and concerns with one another and contacted their families to tell them about their departure.

Rose picked up the telephone to call her father and tell him about this new opportunity and her desire to take it. "Hello, Father?"

"Hello, Rose. How's my favorite daughter?"

"I'm swell. I've got some news for you."

"What is it, Rose?"

"I've been asked to serve in a new overseas unit with the USO. I'm so excited about it."

"What will you be doing, Rose?"

"Traveling around entertaining the servicemen! Doesn't it sound great?"

"Entertaining the servicemen? How?"

"As the reigning USO Queen in the USO shows."

"Oh, what do you have to do? Sing?"

"I don't think so," Rose laughed. "I don't think they'd want me to sing. I just have to wear a pretty gown and smile a lot."

"I bet that there is more to it than that, Rose."

"Whatever it is, Father, I am excited to be a part of if. I'm ready for a new challenge. Really ready!"

"I'm very happy for you, Rose," said her father. "It sounds like a fun opportunity for you. How many weekends will you be gone?"

"Lots of weekends."

"How will you keep up with your school work?"

"Oh, I—I'm taking a break from school."

"What?" her father's tone quickly changed.

"It's just for one semester. I really want to do this father! Please understand. I promise that I'll go back to nursing school after this one semester. I really want to help out the servicemen. I need a change right now, but only for a short while."

"OK. You have my blessing. But promise me that you will go back to nursing school."

"I promise!"

"When will you be leaving?"

"In a few weeks. Can you come out to see me off?" asked Rose. "You promised that when you were feeling better you would come."

"Well, I suppose I could," said her father. "Yes, you can count it!" he quickly decided. "That would be nice."

"I'll see you soon then?"

"OK, Rose. I'll see you as soon as I can get there."

⋘⋘⋘

Conrad arrived a few days before Rose had to leave. She was so anxious to see him she could hardly contain herself.

"I'm so glad that you came all the way out here to Baltimore," Rose said to her father. "There is so much that I want you to see. I'd like to give you a tour around the nursing school first."

127

"That would be great!"

Rose took her father all around the school, showing him where she had her classes and catching him up on the life that she had made for herself so far away from home.

She also gave him a tour of the hospital. This was very impressive. St. Mary's Hospital was well known all over the country for their excellence in research. It was also the largest hospital in the country.

"This is quite a place," commented her father.

"Yes, it's a very large place. It took me awhile to learn my way around and to feel comfortable. I was lucky to have gotten such a nice roommate like Betty."

"Are you ready to have some lunch?" asked Rose.

"You bet! Where's a good place to eat?"

"I'd like to eat here at the hospital cafeteria if you don't mind. I eat here often."

"The food must be pretty good!"

"The food is very good. I think you'll like the variety."

"You know Rose, I feel much better about you being out here so far away from home now that I've been able to come out and see everything. Now I'll be able to picture it in my mind when I'm back home thinking about you. Thanks for prompting me to come. This is very helpful."

"You should have come sooner."

"I know, but I haven't felt very good since your mother passed away."

"I understand. I try to keep very busy here which helps me get on with my life much faster," explained Rose. "But not a day goes by when I don't think about her."

"Me too," her father agreed. "Your mother would be so proud of you, Rose. You've grown up so much!"

"Thanks. That makes me feel good."

"Coming out here makes me realize just how well you have done on your own. Even though I miss your mother so much, and I miss you being so far from home, I see that you are mature enough to make your own decisions. If you decide not to come back home after you finish school, I'll understand. I'm beginning to understand a lot of things."

"Thanks, Father."

"Thank you for spending time with me before you're off again on a new adventure. You are adventurous Rose, I'll give you that!"

Rose and her father enjoyed their special time together. He seemed to have changed. She saw something in him that she had never seen before, but she wasn't sure just exactly what it was.

⊷⊷⊷

The time had come for Rose to leave with her special service unit. Rose and her father rode with one of the other nurses that had her own car and drove to Annapolis. Conrad enjoyed the girls and their enthusiasm for their new adventure. He realized that it was good for him to get off the farm and come to Maryland. It gave him a fresh outlook on life as well.

As they pulled into the Navy base there were "WELCOME CADET NURSES" signs posted everywhere. They were directed to the main office for check-in.

As they passed by the lobby, Rose spotted a bulletin that was posted regarding all of the service men that were MISSING IN ACTION. Rose walked right past it before she realized that maybe she should stop and take a look at it. She picked up the pages and thumbed through them, one-by-one, until she got to the "W" section. There at the bottom of the page she read:

"Adam M. Waterman #13043167 T41 43 A, 3138 Oakford Ave., Baltimore MD P. Declared *missing in action*."

Rose called out, "Father, come over here quickly!"

"What is it, Rose?"

"I've found Adam's name on the this list here on the bulletin board. He's missing, Father, he's missing!"

"Adam is *missing in action*?"

"Yes! That explains why I haven't heard from him lately! Why couldn't someone have contacted me? His parent's could have called me!"

"I don't know why, Rose."

Rose reached out for her father. Conrad wrapped his arms around his daughter and he held her tightly until she could get a hold of herself.

"Come on Rose," prompted her father. "You have to go now. I'll try to keep in touch with the Navy and I'll get word to you as soon as I find out something."

Slowly, they walked to the point of dispatch. Everyone was somber. All chatter had ceased, enthusiasm had waned, and only long faces and silence surrounded them. The atmosphere had taken on a different flavor.

They were transported out onto the runway in jeeps. Conrad was allowed to ride along. They were about to board a C-47 cargo plane that had been specially arranged to fly the USO entertainment unit up and down the coast.

Conrad got out of the jeep, and he stood beside it waiving goodbye to his daughter. As Rose walked toward the plane, she found a smile for her father that communicated her strength and courage.

"Be strong my daughter," Conrad whispered to her as he blew her a kiss.

Rose turned to look at her father as she walked up the steps to the plane. She blew him a kiss back and then went inside.

Conrad got into the jeep to begin his long journey back home.

With a massive lift of energy, the cargo plane took off into the sky. Most of the girls were filled with great anticipation of what they would experience during their service in this unit, but Rose could not stop thinking about Adam. She was so upset to have learned that he was missing in action. She wished that she had more information about it and tried to figure out how she could find out more.

An officer sat down in the seat behind her.

Rose turned around to look at the officer and asked, "Sir, is there any way to find out more information about the men who have been declared *missing in action?*"

"Is there someone in your family that is *missing in action?*"

"I have a very good friend that's missing," replied Rose.

"It is my understanding that only family members may be given any more information than what is posted on the bulletin board back at the base," said the officer. "You might have one of his family members contact the Navy office for more information about his search and rescue. That's about all that I can tell you, unless you are his fiancée."

"No, not exactly," said Rose sheepishly.

"I'm sorry. I'm sure that they are doing everything that they can to try to find him," said the officer.

"Thank you," said Rose as she turned back around in her seat feeling a bit foolish for asking.

Immediately, Rose began to write a letter back to her father to ask him if he could contact the Waterman family to see if they knew anything about Adam. This occupied her thoughts for the duration of the flight to the South Pacific.

Realizing that she had been so pre-occupied with thoughts about Adam, Rose turned toward the girl that was sitting next to her on the plane and introduced herself.

"Hi, my name is Rose. I'm so sorry. I haven't been very polite."

"I'm Kate. It is nice to meet you. I haven't been very polite either. I'm a little nervous about this whole thing."

"Me too," said Rose. "Especially now that I've just found out that a very good friend of mine is *missing in action!*"

"Wow, that doesn't sound good," said Kate. I hope that they find him soon!"

"Thanks. So do I!"

After what seemed like a very long flight, the airplane wheels came down with a loud thud. Rose sensed that they were about to land. The big cargo plane was slowing down and circling the sky for the proper angel for the landing. Rose was frantically chewing on her gum to keep her ears from popping. They circled around one more time and then the plane dropped down slowly out of the sky to land. They had made it!

Looking out the window Rose leaned over to Kate and said, "Look at the trees here. They're so different from the ones back home. This is really going to be an experience!"

"Yes, those are palm trees," said Kate. "They're tropical trees. It will be so beautiful here and I think that you are going to be my roommate while we are here."

"That would be fine with me," agreed Rose. "I'll look forward to getting to know you better. It's been a long trip. I've been worrying about my friend the entire time. I'm so glad that we are finally here!"

The plane slowly came to a complete stop.

Everyone got off the plane and was escorted to their quarters to get settled in for their stay.

৶৶৶

The first show that they put on the following evening was called "IN THE GROOVE." It turned out to be a huge success. They were a big hit with the GIs right from the start.

They performed on a big stage that was decorated with American flags. There were a lot of lights and a lot of GIs. A pianist was set up on the right hand side of the stage. There was a small six-piece band behind the girls. It consisted of a sax player, three trumpet players, a bass player, and a drummer. A very handsome Master of Ceremonies conducted the entire show.

Rose was introduced as the USO Queen. The GIs went crazy with cheers of approval and lots of clapping and whistling.

Rose thought that being up on the stage in front of all those GIs was very nerve-racking. She hoped that she would eventually get used to it and begin to enjoy it.

The entertainment crew brought along a piano called the Victory Piano. It traveled everywhere with the group. This piano was especially designed to accompany the troops in the field. It came in an olive-drab case, and it was very light and transportable.

The shows became better and better as they presented more of them. They were very successful in raising the morale of the soldiers. The war was becoming more and more intense, and their morale would waiver.

In between shows, the girls liked to just kick back and relax, reading mail from home and visiting with one another. They got to know each other very well and enjoyed sharing things with one another.

Kate quickly thumbed through the pile of mail. "You've received a letter from home, Rose!" she announced.

"I did?" she answered. "Quick, let me have it!"

Kate handed her the letter, and Rose swiftly opened it up to see who it was from.

Dear Rose,

After writing to Adam's parents, I've received a letter in return. I thought that I'd better get word to you right away. I know that you've been so terribly worried about him.

He was on the ship called the USS Lexington. A Japanese submarine has torpedoed it and it has sunk in the Pacific. They are still not sure if there are any survivors. The details are very sketchy. Some of the men died at sea, but they still think that some may have made it to shore in lifeboats.

There is a rescue mission going on right now. Pray that they find survivors soon. Time is running out.

Love,
Your Father

"Oh Kate," said Rose as she folded up the letter and drew it close to her heart. "We've got to pray that they find Adam soon!"

ক্ষিক্ষিক্ষি

Back at the Navy headquarters there was a great strategic plan underway. The search for the missing men was diligent and thorough. There was a Special Force assigned to this rescue operation that was indeed one of the best that they had. Their mission was to find these men before the enemy did. The war department knew that in many cases these missing in action soldiers became prisoners of war. Then they were at a great lose in furnishing families with any information, until the country that had captured them decided to release information.

Identification was difficult because all too often the man's dog tags were missing. Men would loose their tags in bathhouses or when working, and they would forget to report the loss. Some units required their men to carry their name, rank and serial number on a piece of paper in their pockets, but that would easily get lost as well.

Rose was feeling helpless in the search for Adam. These feelings were familiar to her when her mother was ill back home, and she was so far away at school. In times like these, there was only one thing for her to rely on, and that was her faith in God. She had to completely trust Him.

The war was taking its toll on everybody's lives. Rose realized, along with thousands of other Americans, that all they could do was to pray—and wait!

CHAPTER 12: WHISPERING HOPE

The special rescue team landed on shore where the intelligence division had calculated that they might find the men from the *USS Lexington*. The weather conditions were not good. It was storm season and any hope to find survivors was quickly fading.

The intelligence division reported enemy occupancy in the area, so the rescue soldiers were equipped for battle as well. They also carried first aid equipment and radios to get help into the area quickly if they needed it. This made their backpacks very heavy.

The search continued for several days, and there was no sign of the missing men. The temperatures were exceptionally low for this time of year, and the rescue team was becoming increasingly frustrated.

Intense artillery began to go off just over the hill from where they were searching. The rescue team found themselves under sporadic fire, which totally caught them by surprise. They swiftly switched from the search mode to a defense mode and ran in different directions as they had been trained to do in a situation like this.

One soldier in particular ran to take cover in a nearby clump of brush that surrounded a hill. He got down on his hands and knees, and he began to dig a trench with his bare hands. As he relentlessly dug down deeper into the earth, he heard a voice calling for help a few feet away in the brush. Quickly, he climbed out of the hole, and he used his hands to clear away the brush. There he found a man, wounded and hiding.

"I've been found!" cried the soldier.

"Were you on the *USS Lexington*?" asked the rescue soldier.

"Yes, and I've been shot during this attack by the enemy. Be careful! They're all around us," said the wounded soldier.

"Let me get you into this trench for cover," said the rescue soldier as he hoisted him up and into the hole that he had dug into the ground.

"Man, I'm glad to see you!" said the injured man.

"I'm glad to see you too," replied the rescuer. "We'd almost given up on finding anyone here. We were just about to move on. What's your name?"

"Adam Waterman," said the soldier. "Watch out! The enemy is all over the place!"

Enemy fire darted through the air above them.

"Yes. I know. We've got to get out of here before we both get killed! Your leg needs some special attention. I'll go back and get some supplies, but for right now I'll wrap a piece of cloth tightly around your leg to get the bleeding stopped. You're bleeding badly!"

The soldier reached into his pocket for a strip of cloth from his medical supplies and wrapped it firmly around Adam's leg where it was bleeding.

"There, that should hold you awhile," he said. "I'll be right back to get you fixed up and ready to move out."

The rescue soldier took off running out of the hole. He was attempting to reach another soldier who was carrying more medical supplies. Heavy fire went off from all directions. He was shot down. Another rescue soldier pulled him off into some nearby bushes. Adam could see all that was happening from the hole in which he was lying. His heart sank.

Adam was determined to reach the soldier that had helped him. He pulled himself up and out of the trench while holding on to his injured leg. He hobbled over to the brush where the soldier was lying. He knelt down on the ground. He could see that he was seriously injured. The bleeding was heavy. He was gasping for breath.

"You've got to hang on," Adam encouraged. "I'll get help!"

"I'll try," he said. "But if I don't make it, I hope you do. No sense both of us going down."

With those last words, he lay his head down, and he died.

Adam couldn't belive what had just happened. It had all happened so fast! His head was spinning, and his leg was hurting badly. Adam turned over the soldier's dog tags and read the name. They read, Wayne Johnson, US Army, Special Forces.

The name Wayne Johnson sounded so familiar to Adam. He quickly recalled where he had heard that name before. He had heard it from Rose. It was her special Wayne Johnson from Apple Grove. Brave man, he thought. He saved my life, but how will I ever tell Rose? He looked around to see if he was in any immediate danger of enemy fire, and he worked his way back to the trench that Wayne had put him in to save his life.

Heavy fire began to break out again, only this time it seemed as if they were much closer. Adam crouched down deeper into the hole, hoping that no one would see him. He pulled out his pocket Bible and opened it up. He was grasping for strength beyond his own physical means.

Adam looked up out of the trench for a moment. The gun-fire continued to echo over his head. He crawled back down into the hole and decided to read more from his Bible.

The shooting stopped after several long hours. The enemy had surrendered to the Special Forces rescue team. Adam was able to climb out of the trench to be rescued. They radioed for an Army helicopter to airlift him out of there. Adam received the medical attention that he needed for his leg. He was flown to a Navy hospital for recovery. That day on the battlefield had changed his life forever!

❦❦❦

As Adam spent a number of days on his back lying in the hospital bed, he had an abundance of time to think. He couldn't stop thinking about Rose. He wanted to know where she was and what she was doing. He felt very fortunate to be alive, and he wanted nothing more than to be with Rose. His entire outlook on life had begun to change.

For once in his life, he knew exactly what he wanted, and he couldn't wait any longer to get it.

Adam got up onto his feet with the help of crutches, and he began to walk down the hospital hallway. He parked himself out in front of the nurse's station.

"Hey, is there someone here that can help me locate a friend back home?" Adam asked.

"Yes, Mr. Waterman, I can help you," replied a kind nurse. "Who would you like to find?"

"I'd like to call a Mr. Conrad Krueger back in Apple Grove, Iowa."

"I'll try to get that information for you," volunteered the nurse.

"I can't wait for very long. My leg is still pretty sore."

"Can I get you a chair?" suggested the nurse.

"That would be fine."

Adam sat down in the chair. He kept wondering where Rose was and if she had forgotten about him by now. It wasn't too long and the nurse had found the telephone number for Adam.

"Hello, Mr. Krueger, this is Adam Waterman calling. How are you?"

"Adam, you've been rescued! Where are you?"

"I'm in a Navy hospital recovering from a gun shot wound. I'm doing well, but I need to find Rose. Do you know where she is?"

"Rose has joined a special USO unit as a Cadet Nurse. She is traveling up and down the coast entertaining the GIs."

"Entertaining the GIs?" Adam sounded surprised.

"Yes, that's right."

"Do you know where she is right now?"

"I'm not sure which location she is at this very minute, but I know that they are scheduled to fly back to the South Pacific next week to do more shows. Maybe you could check with the USO to get a more accurate itinerary."

"How often do you hear from her?"

"Usually once a week. I'll send a telegram today and let her know that you've been found. She'll be thrilled!"

"That's OK Mr. Krueger," said Adam. "I'd like to surprise her. I've got something important to tell her."

"OK, Adam. If that's what you want. Thanks for calling. I've made several attempts to get information about you for Rose, but I haven't been very successful."

"Did Rose ask you to do that?"

"Yes, she's been very worried about you."

"Worried about me?"

"Yes, and I'm glad you're safe too."

"Me too," agreed Adam. "Thanks for the information."

"Goodbye, Adam."

The duration of Adam's recovery period was spent trying to figure out how to get in touch with Rose. He worked very hard on his physical therapy, and in a short amount of time, he was back on his feet again. Searching for Rose greatly motivated him to get well and to get out of the hospital as soon as possible.

The day of his discharge from the hospital finally came. Adam waited patiently for the nurse to come into his room to let him sign the discharge papers.

"I see that you're very anxious to leave, Mr. Waterman," observed the nurse. "You've received a telegram from Apple Grove, Iowa."

Adam quickly took it from the nurse to read it.

Dear Adam,

I thought that you'd like to know what has happened to Rose. I've just received word that her USO cargo plane had to make an emergency landing while on route to the South Pacific. It is thought to have gone down in the mountains of Papua New Guinea. There have been hundreds of planes that have gone down in these mountains in the past and they have never been found. I need your help! Please see what you can do to find Rose!

Conrad Krueger

Now Adam's determination to find Rose was even greater. He felt extreme guilt that he had not gotten on his feet sooner to find her before this had happened. Now, he wasn't sure if he would ever see her again!

The staff at the hospital seemed more than understanding that day. The nurse took him down to the office, and they found the telephone number of the missing plane division.

"I'd like to speak to Lieutenant Colonel Thomas J. Rossburn please," said Adam in a confident voice.

He was the commanding officer of the missing persons division for the US Navy.

"Hello, this is Lieutenant Rossburn speaking."

"Lieutenant Rossburn, this is Adam Waterman, the Navy officer recovered from the *USS Lexington* sinking."

"Oh, yes, I heard about your rescue. Have you made a full recovery?"

"Yes sir, I have. But I have a favor to ask you."

"What can I do for you today?" asked the Lieutenant.

"I'm trying to locate a friend that went down in a USO plane on route to the South Pacific. How can I find out about the search for survivors?" asked Adam.

"You'll need to call the central divisional officer. I'll give you his number and he can inform you about the situation," said the Lieutenant.

"Thank you very much," said Adam.

"I apologize for not being more helpful."

"You've pointed me in the right direction. That is what I needed," said Adam.

"Good luck, Waterman!"

"Thank you, sir."

Adam had much greater luck talking with the central divisional officer. He was able to give him a list of crash sites that they were considering investigating. This division had quick access to many records, and they gave Adam some of the latest information, since he was a Navy officer in good standing.

Adam hung up the telephone, and he knew exactly what he needed to do. He quickly gathered his things and headed for New Guinea!

CHAPTER 13: OH, PROMISE ME

Papua New Guinea was a country where the people spoke in several hundred tribal languages. Adam headed to a village called Manumu. It belonged to a group called the Mountain Koiari. They spoke their own language. Very few people spoke English in Papua New Guinea.

Adam got off the plane at Manumu, and he located the village leader.

He asked the village leader, "Do you know of any planes that have gone down in the mountain area just recently?"

The village leader replied, "There is a *balus* (balus means plane in Melanesian Pidgin English) a four hour trek from the village."

"How do you know this?" asked Adam.

"There are several missing aircraft in the area. Many of these missing aircraft are not really missing. The people of the village already know of them. Because the US Army has not asked them, they don't offer this information," said the village leader. "They choose not to get involved."

Adam graciously thanked the village leader and set out on the long trek to find the plane that went down in the mountains in hopes of finding Rose. His backpack held several days worth of food, along with a medical kit for injuries. He also brought along a radio to call for help if he needed it. A special rescue team had promised to send backup. Thankfully, he did not have to worry about any kind of enemy combat. There was no fighting going on in this area.

The rest of the day was spent unsuccessfully searching and walking. Light rain fell as he prodded on. The sun was not far off from setting for the day.

The first thing that Adam decided to do was to locate a good spot to set up his tent. He walked until he found a fairly level area of ridge suitable for sleeping without rolling down the mountainside. The villagers had warned him about the changeable weather patterns. He decided to play if safe and lay down some plastic before setting up his tent. Then he put posts in the ground and began setting up the rest of the tent. His tent was tightly enclosed on all sides and he was able to build a small fire out in front of it. He placed a pot to simmer over the fire in preparation to make some hot cocoa. Supper consisted of C rations and carrots.

Just as the early evening darkness fell down around him there was a great flapping of wings and several loud shrieks. More and more shrieks were heard, one after another. The shrieks were very high pitched like screams from a horror movie. Adam stretched his head out of his tent to look to see what it was. It was giant bats! The bats flew closer and closer to his tent. Adam began to wonder if he was going to be their supper. After about an hour of circling his tent, they began to depart. Things came to a complete calmness and Adam was glad. It was the end of a very long day!

The next morning, after the heavy fog lifted that encircled the campsite, Adam was able to see a propeller in the distance. He began to clear away the brush. He cut small trees away with his machete. Making his way through the tangled vines and the thick brush, he came across another part of a propeller and other plane parts. His heart began to race with excitement accompanied by fear. He continued to search for clues and pieces of the plane. As he worked his way down the mountain slope, he kept losing his balance. It became jagged and rugged going down. Adam was glad that he had his heavy gloves on to grab hold of the vines to help him keep his footing.

As he inched his way closer and within the proximity of the wreckage, he saw the fuselage and fragments of the cockpit sprawled out over the brush. Shoes, boots, helmets and other items of clothing were strung out across the area. Adam wondered if the next thing that he would see would be bodies. His heart began pounding against the walls of his chest.

As he continued to walk, he came across the instrument panel of the airplane. It was broken into a million pieces. His heart skipped another beat as he realized that possibly no one could have survived this terrible crash. He began to feel anxious about what he soon might find. He hoped that it wouldn't be too uncomfortable to witness and that Rose wasn't in this sprawled out rubble.

The crash site covered a piece of ground that was about forty to sixty yards from north to south, and about one-hundred-seventy from east to west. Adam came upon the tail fin and picked it up off of the ground using all of the strength that he could muster. Upon the bottom of the tail fin he found some serial numbers that identified the aircraft. Beside the serial number there was an American flag. This was a welcomed sight.

Adam dropped the tail fin and reached deep into his pocket for a piece of paper. He held the piece of paper next to the serial numbers on the tail fin to see if it matched, and read them out loud.

"Tail number 2-53099. I FOUND IT!" shouted Adam. "I FOUND HER PLANE!"

Now, he needed to find bodies. He was not certain that he would find anyone alive, but he hadn't given up hope just yet. Adam pressed on in search of Rose.

Adam kept searching through lunch. He snacked on a few crackers and pieces of dried fruit that he had brought along. The day was warm but it was beginning to cloud over and become a bit cooler.

As he walked a greater distance around the crash site, he found a parachute. Lifting the parachute up in his hands, he discovered that it had been deployed. It was intertwined with roots and branches. Adam was becoming more hopeful that he would find some survivors, but all of this really puzzled Adam. He speculated that the people on the airplane must have parachuted out before the plane crashed. This made him think that there were indeed survivors. But where could they be?

His back was beginning to hurt and he was shivering from the cool air. He worked his way back to the tent and started to settle in for another night. He found it hard to break for nightfall but decided that it was necessary due to his fatigue and the darkness. As evening approached, the bats began to shriek again as they had done the night before on the mountain. Adam tried to ignore them this time, and he ate his rations.

He pulled out his pocket Bible. His Bible had become a great source of strength through all that he had experienced as a result of the war. This was how he was able to withstand being a soldier. He found himself in circumstances that he had never dreamed that he would be in. After he read a comforting passage, he dozed off to sleep. He was exhausted from searching all day.

The sun came up, and Adam was ready to continue searching for Rose. He went back to the crash site and tried to decide which direction they might have headed if they did survive with parachutes. Adam searched the area in all directions, moving further and further out around the wreckage. Time was running out, Adam thought. They couldn't survive too long in these mountains with limited supplies. His food supply was getting low as well.

Hours passed and Adam was getting discouraged. He knelt down by a large rock, prayed and rested for a few minutes. He stood up on his feet and began to climb down the mountainside to the west. He walked until the sun set in the west. Disappointed in his progress, he set up camp for another night. He got out his gear. Just as he pulled his tent out of his backpack, he glanced over the mountain, and he saw smoke rising up from the trees. Immediately, he stuffed his tent back in his backpack, and he headed off to where the smoke was billowing up over the treetops.

There in the middle of the clearing behind the trees was a group of people huddling together around a campfire trying to keep warm.

Adam raced over to the group and said, "Hey, are you survivors of the USO plane crash?"

Everyone turned to look at Adam, and they all stood up and cheered, "We've been rescued! Hooray!"

There were tears of joy as they came up to greet Adam. He tried to calm them down to ask them about Rose. He began looking around the crowd for her. His eyes searched through the people that were trying to talk to him about their rescue.

"Has anybody seen a woman named Rose?" he frantically called out through the crowd.

He got no response.

"I'm looking for a woman named Rose Krueger?" he called out again. "Does anyone know who she is?"

They only shook their heads in response to his call. It seemed as if no one knew her. He was starting to perspire.

Suddenly he spotted a woman coming toward him. She was trying to make her way through the crowd. Adam used his arms to gently make his way through the people to get closer to her. He finally reached her, and he saw that it was Rose! He welcomed her in his arms and held her tightly.

"I've finally found you!" said Adam, as he embraced her in his arms as if he'd never let her go. "You're alive! Do you feel OK? Do you think that you have any broken bones?"

"No, I'm fine. I was so lucky!"

"You really were. I went through all the wreckage and when I saw it, I wasn't sure how anyone could have survived that crash."

"The crew was great. They reacted in all the right ways to save our lives."

"I'm so thankful!" said Adam as he gave her another hug.

Rose began to cry, "You've rescued me again Adam. I love you!"

"I love you too, Rose!"

"How did they find you, Adam? The last information that I had been given was that you were *missing in action*."

"I was rescued off the pacific shore after the *Lexington* sunk. A group of us made it to shore in lifeboats. Rose, I know that this is not the best time to tell you this, but there is something you should know."

"What is it, Adam?"

"I was rescued by a soldier named Wayne Johnson."

"Wayne Johnson from back home?"

"Yes. He saved my life, but he lost his in the process. He was a brave man."

"Oh, Adam. I don't know what to say." She lowered her head for a moment of silence.

"Adam, we've got to help the others. That's what Wayne would want me to do.

He gently reached out to lift up her chin. "Rose, be brave as well. That is also what Wayne would want you to do."

Adam had found that some of the people had more serious injuries as he quickly checked everyone over before he radioed for help.

"Rose, while we are waiting for the rescue team to get here, I'm going to need you to assist me. We need to get them ready to airlift out of here. Can you help me? Your nursing skills will come in handy."

"Sure, Adam. What would you like me to do?"

"There's a man over there that has an injured leg. There is also a woman over there that needs some kind of a splint on her arm. Can you help them both?"

"No problem," she said.

"I'll continue to see what is necessary here, Rose and I'll let you know. Stand by for further details."

Adam and Rose made a good team, trying to make everyone as comfortable as possible while they waited for more help to arrive.

"Rose, I think that we have everyone taken care of for now. Let's go for a walk. I need to talk to you in private."

They walked a short distance into the wood, and he held her close.

"Rose, I don't ever want to lose you again!"

"And I don't ever want to lose you either," she agreed.

"Rose, will you marry me?"

Rose looked deep into his weary eyes and said, "Yes, Adam, I will!"

Adam embraced her in his arms with a thankful heart that she was safe.

"We need to get back," he said. "Help should be here soon."

Within a few hours they were all airlifted off the mountain and flown to a hospital. Adam never left Rose's side during her checkup at the hospital.

The doctor gave Rose a clean bill of health with the exception of a few bumps and bruises.

As they both walked out the hospital door, Adam said, "Let me take you back to Iowa, Rose. Your father will be anxious to see you."

" I'm really ready to go home, Adam! I never thought that I'd hear myself say that, but I've had about all the adventure that I want for a life time!"

"Let's get married in the Lutheran Church in Apple Grove," suggested Adam.

"Yes, Adam, that would be perfect!"

"I'll get a job back in Apple Grove and we can settle down there, too!"

"That sounds wonderful, Adam, but do you think that you would be happy living in the Mid-West?"

"I love the Mid-West! I'll even consider becoming a Lutheran!"

"Wow, my father will be surprised!" said Rose. "You know, the best part of this whole thing is that I'm finally at peace with going back to Apple Grove. Yes, that is what I desire."

The Navy and the USO unit dismissed the both of them, and they went back to Iowa to be married. Adam received a number of awards for his courage in his successful rescue of the USO plane crash survivors. He was also promoted to First Lieutenant with an honorable discharge. He was a hero in the eyes of the military and in the eyes of Rose.

CHAPTER 14: I LOVE YOU TRULY

It was a day to celebrate! Excitement filled the air in the Lutheran Church in Apple Grove, Iowa. This was the church that Rose had grown up in. It was a quaint little church that began in her grandparent's home back in 1856.

This church was the first Lutheran Church in Benton County. Apple Grove wasn't even a town until 1867. You could see the big church steeple from far off into the distance. It was topped with a wooden cross. Under the cross was a bell tower. The bells rang out a beautiful song across the countryside on this wedding day.

The sun was shining in at just the perfect angle to set aglow the beautiful stained glass windows in the church. A glistening ray of light dazzled the inside of the church that day as if they were receiving heavenly approval for this occasion.

The wedding party began to arrive. The men waited in a room just off the sanctuary. The bridesmaids met Rose in the basement of the church to get dressed in their gowns.

Adam had asked Kirky to come back from Baltimore to be his best man. He also asked a cousin of Rose's to stand up for him, since Rose had picked two bridesmaids, Lilly and her college roommate, Betty.

Rose and Lilly had spent the entire day before decorating the church. They tied bows on the pews down the aisle, and they decorated with a lot of flowers. Rose brought in her mother's china from the farmhouse that she had always used for special occasions for the reception.

Rose had a lot of help preparing for the wedding from the many cousins that lived in the area. They loved to celebrate special occasions, and this was definitely one of them.

All of the relatives were anxious to meet this Adam Waterman that they all had heard so much about. They knew that he must be somebody very special to marry Rose.

Rose was hurrying to get her last earring on in the basement with her bridesmaids when she remembered that she had forgotten something.

"Lilly, I'm so nervous! I can't remember where I left the blue garter that I was going to wear under my dress," said Rose in a panic.

"Oh yes, you need something old and something blue. Is that right, Rose?"

"Yes, I'm wearing my mother's old pearls, but I've lost my blue garter!" said Rose.

"I'll run upstairs to see if anyone has seen it up there," said Lilly as she raced toward the door.

Lilly hurried up the wrong stairway and right into the room where Adam and his groomsmen were waiting.

"Oh my goodness!" squealed Lilly. "I took the wrong stairs. I'm looking for Rose's blue garter. Has anyone seen it?"

The men got quite a laugh out of this. They began to joke and tease Adam about it.

"Now we know what Rose will be wearing," Kirky taunted.

"Well, we haven't seen anything like that up here," Adam told Lilly.

"Rose is very worried about having something blue with her as she comes down the aisle. It's traditional, I guess," said Lilly.

"Here, I've got something blue," said Adam as he reached into his suit pocket. "Give her this."

Adam handed Lilly his pocket Bible that he had carried with him in the Navy. It had a blue velvet cover.

"All right," agreed Lilly. "Maybe this will do."

Lilly quickly left the room as fast as she had come into it and headed back down the stairs to give the Bible to Rose.

"Here, Rose," Lilly said handing her the blue-covered Bible. "Adam said that you may carry this down the aisle instead of the blue garter that you're missing."

"Oh, his pocket Bible," commented Rose as she drew it close to her heart. "This is perfect!"

Rose tucked the small Bible underneath her bouquet of flowers, and she called for the girls to come and line up for the processional.

At the back of the church Rose joined her father. He was all dressed up in a gray and white pin-stripped suit.

"You look beautiful, Rose," Conrad whispered in her ear. "I'm so proud of you! I'm also very happy that you've found a man like Adam."

"Thank you," said Rose as she pulled back her veil of lovely, soft lace.

"Rose, I have something to tell you."

"What is it, Father?"

"I'm sorry for all of the pressure that I put on you in the past concerning the church and who to marry. Will you forgive me?"

"Why yes, of course," she said.

"I see that you've grown up into such a nice young woman all by yourself, and I really like Adam!" he said.

"Adam mentioned that he would be willing to become a Lutheran," she said with a smile.

"That is a bonus, Rose!"

"But, the best part, Father, is that I am at peace with coming back to settle down here in Apple Grove because of what I've been through."

" I never dreamed that you'd come back home, and by your own decision!" Conrad smiled and began to slowly usher his daughter in from the back of the church.

As they walked down the aisle, Conrad was having mixed feelings. He felt joy and sadness because today he was giving away his only daughter, forever.

Rose was dressed in a beautiful gown. Her veil was crowned with seed pearls and rhinestones that framed her lovely face. She carried a shower bouquet of white roses and bouvardia. Her gown was a fitted bodice that buttoned down the back. It had a ruffled bertha and a lace yoke. Her long sleeves ended in points over the wrists. Her skirt of tiered ruffles extended into a junior train. This gown greatly enhanced her tiny figure.

The bridesmaids followed Rose to the altar in pink and blue taffeta gowns. They carried cascade bouquets of Talisman roses.

Adam reached out his arm for Rose to take hold of, as they approached the front of the church.

Adam leaned over to Rose and whispered in her ear, "I have one more surprise for you!"

"I wonder what it could be!" she said as her eyes brightened.

"You'll find out later," he said grinning from ear to ear.

"You're just full of surprises aren't you Adam?" Rose whispered back to him. "That's why I love you…truly!"

The wedding party all took their places up in the front of the church. Reverend Winters carried out the wedding ceremony in a traditional Lutheran way, leading the congregation in some traditional Lutheran hymns.

Reverend Winters introduced them as Mr. and Mrs. Adam Waterman, husband and wife. Adam and Rose turned to face one another as they held hands in front of the church. Adam reached over and gave her a kiss. They walked down the aisle, gazing upon one another with great pleasure and joy in their hearts.

A reception followed in the church basement. Adam and Rose were asked to stand behind the wedding cake for a picture before it was served. The wedding cake was unforgettable. It had heart shaped tiers with red tea roses nestled on a blanket of creamy white frosting that topped this magnificent red velvet cake. Red velvet petite fours in miniature versions of the wedding cake elegantly decorated the table. This cake truly captured the essence of this beautiful occasion.

It was time for Rose to throw the bouquet to all of the unmarried ladies in the crowd. They all gathered in hopes of being the lucky one to catch the bouquet. Rose turned to face the opposite direction of the group of ladies and lowered her arm down to toss the flowers up, back and over her shoulder in the traditional manner. The other hand covered her eyes so that she couldn't see where she was tossing it.

Rose gave it a quick, hard toss. Her throw somehow went awry, and it sailed off in the wrong direction, hitting Adam right in the side of the head! He reached down and picked up the bouquet with a chuckle, and the crowd laughed.

"Now Rose, you've done it again!" Adam spoke up over the crowd in a teasing voice. "I sure hope this is the last time you try to throw something here at this church!"

Rose put her hands over her mouth as if she were going to die of embarrassment. "I'm so sorry...really I am!"

"That's OK Rose, I knew when I married you that you couldn't throw very well," said Adam. "Now this time, don't run off!"

"This time I won't!" she said.

Rose was just beginning to collect herself, and the groomsmen came up from behind her and whisked her up over their shoulders and carried her off. They carried her up the basement steps and out the front door of the church, high up over their heads.

"What in the world are you guys doing!" she screamed.

"We're kidnaping the bride!"

"You're what?" she said.

"Kidnaping the bride! Just relax Rose. You're going for a ride."

"Oh no I'm not!" she protested. "Put me down...now!"

"Not yet, Rose. You're ours for awhile."

"Adam! Help!"

"I'm right behind you Rose. I'm coming too!"

"Where are they taking me?"

"I'm not sure. Your cousin said that it's some kind of tradition around here to kidnap the bride and take her off for a while. We'll find out soon. Hang on, honey!"

They carried Rose past the apple orchard and over the bridge into downtown Apple Grove. It wasn't too far, but the ride felt a little bumpy to Rose being up so high in the air.

They carried her into the general store.

"Why are we going in here, guys?"

"You'll see, Rose."

Mr. and Mrs. Smith had wedding presents for them. A variety of household supplies were purchased to get Adam and Rose off to a good start.

"There is one more present out back behind the general store," said Mr. Smith.

Rose and Adam walked out behind the store to see what it was. There was Conrad standing beside a new Mercury.

"Here's the keys," he said. "Congratulations!"

"Father, you shouldn't have!" cried Rose.

"Well, I did, and you two deserve it. I wish you lots of happiness and I'm so glad to have you back in Apple Grove."

The Smith's had some presents on a table inside the store, and they offered free rootbeer to everyone who came in with the bride.

"This is great everyone!" said Rose "Thank you for all of your gifts."

"Now I have a special surprise for Rose," said Adam "Let's get her back to the church and I'll take her to see it next."

If there was one thing to remember about Apple Grove, Iowa, it would be to remember how they celebrated a wedding. This they knew well!

Back at the church there was a special horse and buggy waiting for them out front that was decorated with streamers and fresh flowers. On the back of the coach was a sign that said, JUST MARRIED.

The rest of the people came outside in front of the church, and they tossed white rose petals up in the air at Adam and Rose as they approached the horse and buggy.

Adam turned to address the crowd. "Thank you all for coming to celebrate this special day with Rose and I. We've gone through a lot to get here today and I'm thankful to be alive and I'm thankful for my wife, Rose. We'll be back in a little while. I've got something to show her."

Adam and Rose got inside the buggy. They took off down the road and around the curve to the top of the highest hill by the cemetery that overlooked the farm. The buggy came to a complete stop and Adam got out and went around to help Rose.

"Adam, why are we stopping here?" asked Rose.

"Because the surprise that I have for you is here," he said.

"Out here? What do you mean?"

"Come walk with me to the edge of the hill," he said. "You can see it better."

"See what better?" she asked, more curious than ever.

"Rose, this is my wedding gift to you," Adam said as he stretched out his arms in the direction of the land all around the farm.

"My wedding gift? I don't understand."

"After purchasing the land from your father, the bank that I worked for decided that they didn't want it any more, so I slowly bought it back."

"You're kidding me, right?"

"No. I have been saving it for you—for us."

"Wait a minute. You own the land now?"

"No, we do. We can make this our home and you will have your land to pass on to the next generation."

"What about my father? What will he do?"

"I've already discussed this with him. He has purchased a house in town. He wants us to live on the family farm."

"That's perfect! I can finish nursing school in Cedar City. Oh, Adam, I'm finally home to stay. This is the best wedding gift that you could have possibly given me," she said. "I do love you, truly I do!"

❧❧❧

"That is the most beautiful story that I've ever heard," said Rose as the porch swing slowly came to a stop. "And to think that you named me after my Grandmother Rose makes me feel very special!"

"You are very special!" her mother affirmed. "Now you may open your gift that I have been saving just for your sixteenth birthday."

Her mother handed her a small box that was carefully wrapped in pink paper with a beautiful silver bow. Rose carefully removed the paper. It was a delicate music box. She noticed that it wound up, and she gave it a gentle turn.

"What song does it play, Mother?"

"It plays the *Gazebo Waltz*," she said. "That was your grandparent's favorite waltz. They danced to it in the gazebo the night they first met at the Sweet Corn Festival."

Rose opened up the lid and found a beautiful charm bracelet that held one single charm on it. It was a rose.

"Is this the bracelet that Grandfather Adam bought for Grandmother Rose when they went shopping in Chestertown?" asked Rose.

"Yes, this is the exact one!" said her mother. "Your Grandmother Rose gave me the bracelet and the music box when I was sixteen."

"Oh, Mother this is the best birthday present that I've ever had! Thank you so much!" said Rose.

"You are welcome, Rose. Happy sixteenth birthday! Let's go frost that red velvet cake."

"Now I also know why this red cake is so special," said Rose. "I'll have lots of things to pass on to my family someday."

ROSE'S RED VELVET CAKE

½ cup shortening
1 ½ cups sugar
2 eggs
2 ounces (¼ cup) red food coloring
2 tablespoons cocoa
1 teaspoon salt
1 teaspoon baking soda
1 teaspoon vinegar
1 cup buttermilk
2¼ cups all-purpose flour

Preheat oven to 350 degrees. Cream together the shortening, sugar and eggs until light and fluffy. Slowly blend in the food coloring and cocoa to this mixture. Set aside.

In another bowl, add the salt, baking soda, and vinegar to the buttermilk and mix thoroughly. Add this mixture in thirds, alternately with the flour, to the shortening mixture, beating well after each addition.

Pour the batter into two greased and floured cake pans and bake for 25 to 30 minutes or until done. Cool on wire rack.

ELEGANT FROSTING

3 tablespoons flour
1 cup milk
2 sticks butter (softened to room temperature)
1 cup confectioner's sugar
1 teaspoon vanilla

Cook flour and milk over low heat until thick, stirring constantly. Let cool. Cream together the butter, sugar and vanilla. Add the flour mixture slowly and beat until it is of spreading consistency. Spread between layers of cake, top and sides.

OPTIONAL CREAM CHEESE FROSTING

2 packages cream cheese (3 oz. each), softened
6 tablespoons butter, softened
1 teaspoon vanilla
2 cups sifted powered sugar

Blend all of the ingredients until smooth. Frost cake as desired. This is also a very nice frosting to use on the red cake for cream cheese lovers!

GAZEBO WALTZ

Sue Ellen Willett

A ROSE

A beautiful symbol of love
That represents the one thing that death cannot take…
The memories of our loved ones that have gone before us
And our hope for the future.

SW

The Lord is my light and my salvation.
Psalm 27:1

Printed in the United States
1493800002B/379-402

9 781591 293835